BAQWA PRESENTS: TWO

BAY AREA QUEER WRITERS ASSOCIATION ANTHOLOGY VOLUME 2

M.D. Neu • R.L. Merrill

Liz Faraim • K.S. Trenten

Wayne Goodman • Richard May

Gar McVey-Russell • Vincent Traughber Meis

Michael Alenyikov • Kelliane Parker

ISBN: 978-1-7344700-6-2

Copyright © 2022

Cover Art: Glenn Quigley
Design/Layout: Wayne Goodman

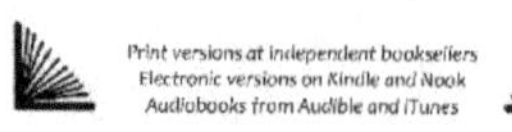

About BAQWA

The Bay Area Queer Writers Association is a group of local writers who support and encourage each other.

The goal of the group is to create a strong visible writing community here in the San Francisco Bay Area. They are based in Silicon Valley, but they have members from all over the Bay Area.

This group is open to anyone who loves to read and wants to help support area authors. You don't have to live in the Bay Area to be a member, you just have to love Queer books and enjoy reading.

For more information, please visit https://baqwawriters.wixsite.com/books

TABLE OF CONTENTS

GIVE ME TWO

Give me two seconds and I can ask a question.

Give me two minutes and I can explain it.

Give me two hours and we can discuss things.

Give me two days and we can get to know each other.

Give me two weeks and I might want to get to know you better.

Give me two months and we will learn together.

Give me two years and you will be in love.

Can you give me two?

–Wayne Goodman

NIGHTINGALE'S HEART

M.D. NEU

Have you ever had a crush on someone you've worked with? I think we all have. As time passed, you finally accepted that a business relationship was all you would ever get, but not today. Not now. This short story is all about crossing lines and taking chances and seeing what happens, for good or for bad. We may not get to explore those choices in real life, but in the safety of these pages, we get to indulge in our fantasies.

Chapter One

The music from the band blasted and played as the fans who filled the arena sang along and cheered. Rahim was glad his ears were protected with the earpiece he wore. Of all the places Aza played, this area was one of the better ones. As was the city. These larger newer venues despite their size were more easily secured. Rahim stood ramrod straight, scanning the area for trouble. Still, his stare would move to Aza, and their full lips, long eyelashes and dark hair. Plus, they always seemed to be surrounded by the scents of orange and ginger, a combination that reminded Rahim of his home growing up. He loved that smell.

The gentle sway of Aza's hips as they moved in time with the words they sang and the music that played could transfix Rahim for hours if he allowed it. The music was nothing he grew up with, well not that his parents would have permitted, but he never did everything his parents instructed. He followed his own path, not only in his tastes of music but in his life and who he loved.

Having traditional parents wasn't easy. They came to the U.S. wanting him and his sisters to have a better life, so some of their old traditions and biases had to change. What was the point of leaving a place in fear if you embraced the same rules and prejudices that you fled? No. He blazed the way for his younger sisters. Softening their parents so they had an easier time as they grew up.

He smiled at the memories.

I'll have to call them and check in.

He shifted his stance; focusing. He examined the surroundings. There were security risks in every corner of the arena and with all these people rushing about, it was hard to ensure Aza's safety. Typically, once Aza was on stage nothing much happened. There was at least one fan per show who tried to sneak backstage or rush the stage to get their hands-on Aza. Rahim or one of this team would have to stop them or physically remove them. Aza never seemed to mind, they loved their fans and always ended up giving the person a quick hug or smile and wink. A little extra something for them to remember the show by. And not just a police or security escort out of the venue.

Aza never even pressed charges, except that one time, which just shows even they have limits.

A voice over his ear piece called his attention; there were two teens that tried to get backstage and were removed.

"East section now clear. Nightingale secure?" Darius asked.

"They're fine. Performing." Rahim responded with a click of his mic.

"Under your eyes I'm sure they are just fine." There was a chuckle then the mic clicked off.

Rahim ignored the comment, his team loved to rib him about Aza, or *Nightingale* as they coded them. If they knew he had any feelings for Aza his team would never say anything, but his team still took great pleasure in giving him shit. He refocused his attention to the stage and all those around; making sure everything and everyone was as it should be.

One breach is all it takes.

Aza had hired Rahim and his team two years back after an incident with a fan's threats. These threats first started out as social media comments and cyber stalking but quickly escalated, especially after Aza blocked them from communicating with them. Sadly, this wasn't a normal fan wanting a kiss or autograph. The guy had mental health issues and was not only a danger to Aza, but to himself. Poor Aza had a fright when they got home and found the guy in their bedroom masturbating while wearing some of Aza's clothes. From what he had learned the encounter was awful and really frightened Aza. An event like that couldn't be easy for someone delicate like Aza. Not only did Aza hire Rahim and his security team, but they hired a security consultant to upgrade their home. A task that Rahim and his team had since taken over and improved. Since then, Aza had entrusted Rahim with all the necessary security measures for their home, when they toured, and for themselves. Despite his hiring and his first few interaction with Aza, most of the time, Rahim worked with Dee, Aza's PA, which was fine, but he still would have liked to spend more time with the singer, like when they were at the events.

Aza needed to be able to focus on their career and their music, so they couldn't fuss around with all the security needs of their home and when they were on tour, or out meeting the public. These moments when Aza was on stage were nice, at least for Rahim.

Rahim remembered those first few weeks and how stressed Aza had been, they hated having to do all the extra steps and really didn't like having the security team around them twenty-four seven. Dee had insisted and Aza finally agreed. Rahim had promised Dee and Aza that he would do everything he could to make sure that he and his team were as invisible as possible. He swore he would be the one to handle Aza personally, never letting anyone else take care of them. Still Aza always seemed nervous and a bit scared around him. Aza was Rahim's responsibility, something he felt deep in his bones. At first he felt as if Aza were another sibling, but as Rahim got to know Aza it became much more. Here was this beautiful, sensitive artist sharing their talent with the world, not able to hurt a fly, who loved everyone. At times Rahim felt that it might not be so much that Aza was delicate, but frustrated that they couldn't take care of themselves. He appreciated that, no adult liked to feel they couldn't handle themselves, or protect themselves, and now having him, a big lunk of a man, around to ensure no one took advantage of them or doing... God only knows what.

No wonder Aza is always so standoffish with me. I wouldn't want me around either. Given how passive Aza is, me being around all the time probably goes against who they are.

Rahim listened to an update from his team as he watched Aza and their surroundings.

It would be nice to enjoy the show. Sit and watch them. Really watch them and see them. Without worrying.

Rahim's gaze narrowed on a man across the stage, standing watching Aza. He wasn't anyone from the crew or the tech team.

"Nancy." Rahim called into his mic. She would be on that side of the stage and she was his number two.

"I see him."

"Let's not make a fuss." Rahim kept his eyes on the stranger. "Keep it friendly."

"Always." Nancy's voice sang out into his ear. "Don't worry, I know how important Nightingale is to you and the rest of us."

Rahim watched as Nancy approached the man standing viewing the show. The guy startled as Nancy began to question him. Without a commotion or even noticed by anyone else, the man and Nancy were gone in an instant.

Nancy was excellent at her job and, because of her size and her sex, she blended in and everyone underestimated her. Sadly, even him, when he interviewed her. Yes, she had been in the military and had more special ops training than Rahim, but he wasn't sure about her. Until he ended up on his ass when he made the mistake of telling Nancy she might not be cut out for his security detail. How he went from standing to floor so quickly impressed him. Even his biggest guy couldn't best him, but Nancy did and she didn't even mess-up her suit. He was glad she knocked him on his ass. The lesson reminded him not to judge people. He hired her on the spot and never looked back. He then promoted her within six months.

And I couldn't be more pleased.

"BG." Nancy's voice filled his ear piece.

"Yep."

"All clear, the guy was maintenance, he wasn't wearing his credentials. Chip and Dale cleared him and sent him on his way."

Rahim chuckled and rubbed his chin as the day's growth of stubble scratched his hand. "You know they don't appreciate being called that."

"I know." Nancy held back her laugh. "That's why I do it."

Rahim shook his head, he checked his watched. He gave another quick glance to Aza on the stage, their movements so graceful and refined. He sighed. It was time to make a round. He walked his area to guarantee everything was as it should be. Unlike Aza, Rahim was the opposite of delicate; in high school he was a defensive lineman. These tight areas and small passageways back stage always made for a crowded fit. And he ripped more jackets then he cared to admit, keeping his neighborhood tailor busy. Aza seemed to glide through all these tight spaces with ease; not him. He didn't mind the claustrophobic feelings in a place like this, it meant that people were restricted in their movements; however, there were places where things could go wrong. That was something he didn't like. And he always wished he and his team had more time to secure these larger venues, but that was never the case. And he had to learn quickly where the problem areas were, where to find them, and how to counter them ensuring he and his team were nimble enough on their feet to handle every eventuality. Luckily, his coach in high school made the whole football team take a dance class, it helped them with their movements and gave them an appreciation for their bodies and how they worked, which helped a great deal. Even after graduation, when he went into the Marines, all those movement exercises paid off.

He moved the mechanics and the rigging out of his way after a quick round and returned to his spot to wait and watch for Aza. It reminded him of some of the places he had served. Talk about tight spaces. There was never enough room when you were stationed in some far-off land, fighting for your country. After his stint in the Marines, and having a tough time transitioning back to civilian life, he put his size and training to use in security.

First, he learned the ropes while working for others. Then after five years he broke out on his own. Starting his own security firm wasn't easy, and at the beginning the work took up all his time and energy, but now he was happy with where the company was, and the reputation they had. Being established like he was, he could take on the roles and responsibilities he wanted, delegating the clients and the tasks he didn't want to do, or was too busy for. People came to him, so he didn't have to find new clients.

Glad my work can speak for itself. Still I have to keep the clients happy and satisfied

Working personally with clients, like Aza, who he chose, were what kept him the happiest. He also kept his A-Team for himself and Aza. He scanned the arena taking in all the features and everything about the building. He really would have loved to have seen this place during the design phase and being built. He nodded and checked his watch again, ensuring he was on schedule. This work was a far cry from the occupation the sensitive kid who wanted to be an architect wanted to do, but life didn't always give you what you wanted. Plus, if he had become an architect, he wouldn't be here watching Aza and getting to bask in their light and personality.

Rahim checked his watch then ran a hand through his hair. The time always seemed to speed by like a bullet firing from a gun. Once fired it was over. However, once the show finished, unlike a gun shot, people were energized and happy, not lifeless and scared.

"BG." Nancy's words broke him once more from his thoughts.

"Go." He responded.

"The show's wrapping up, do you know how many calls Aza's got planned?"

Rahim smirked. His eyes focused on Aza and their dancers. They really did give everything they had to each performance. "Planned or will do?"

"You know what I mean." Nancy chided. "Should we get things ready for the car, and should we contact the team at the hotel? Give them an ETA on Nightingale."

"Yes, and yes." Rahim said. "Let's have everything ready to go. I don't want Aza waiting on us. We don't have to worry about striking anything tonight since they have two more shows here."

"Understood." Nancy clicked off the mic.

"Oh Nancy."

"Yep." She responded.

"I'll see to Nightingale tonight, get them off stage and to the green room." Rahim added. "And I'll get them to the car. You can start the move and have a little break."

"You're the boss." Nancy responded with another click followed by silence

Yep. I'm the boss.

As such he enjoyed these few short moments with Aza alone. Not that they talked much. Aza kept to their inner circle, which Rahim and his team were not part of. In his mind and daydreams they would have conversations. But nothing ever happened between them, not that he didn't hope or fantasize. Based on who Aza seemed to spend personal time with, it appeared Rahim wasn't their type.

Rahim glanced at his watch again.

Good thing I'm used to these late nights.

Chapter Two

The music stopped and the applause grew as the audience chanted and cheered. The noise made it impossible to hear anything. Rahim always found himself clapping along with the crowd once the show finished. It was a habit he never seemed to be able to break.

"Hey, big guy." Aza hurried past to change into their encore outfit. Under the smell of sweat, Rahim still managed to get hints of orange and ginger and his lips tugged up into a smile.

Rahim nodded. This change of Aza's was the most elaborate and hardest for them and the crew to do, but like with his security team, Aza had a strong support team of Costume Professionals that helped them shift from one outfit to the next. The stage crew was equally as professional and fastidious at their jobs.

Big Guy.

At one time, Rahim thought *Big Guy* was a special nickname Aza had for him. Rahim's heart would skip a beat each time. But no. *Big Guy* was how Aza addressed the security team, except for Nancy.

Did they even give Nancy a nickname? I'm not sure.

The crowd continued to cheer and chant Aza's name as everything moved in both slow motion and rapid succession. Right now, his job was to stay out of the way of the crew while keeping an eye on Aza. The change took five minutes thirty-five seconds, that was down from the eight minutes when the tour first started. The transformation always impressed Rahim and part of him wished he could be out there too with the dancers and backup singers, but he didn't have that kind of talent.

Aza walked by in a rush of glitter, they reached out and grabbed Rahim's arm for balance. "Let's give the fans what they want, right Big Guy?" Aza beamed as a fresh wave of orange and ginger broke the scents of grease, dust, and body odor. "One call after this, then I'll take a shower and we can jet. Thanks, Big Guy." Aza added as they and the rest of the dance troupe rushed back out on stage.

Big Guy.

The first week on the job; when Aza called him, Big Guy, Rahim walked taller and with what Nancy called a big dopey grin on his face. He thought maybe there might be something there. A spark, something that could be built on. But when he heard Aza speak to Darius, and Aza called Darius, Big Guy, his heart ached and he knew nothing special existed between them, no matter how much Rahim's heart yearned for it to be otherwise.

After that Rahim thought about switching Aza's security to one of his other leads, but there was something about Aza, and Rahim couldn't bear to do that to them. Rahim continued to do his job, focused on ensuring the client's safety. Keeping their interaction professional and continuing to work mostly with Dee, to stay out of Aza's way and ensure they never had anything to worry about, well at least from a security stand point. Even now, tonight, he did his job, checked in, and ensured everything was ready for Aza's departure. As he waited for Aza to finish their curtain calls he continued to spare prolonged glances at Aza not fully focusing on how the crew and the various support staff were wrapping things up for the night around him.

Each glance he spared to Aza filled with his Hope.

Nancy and his team took to calling him BG because of Aza. He didn't mind, after all he had been called worse; much worse. And the nickname helped to break down some of the professional barriers he and his team had.

He found that morale improved and people worked harder when they saw you as human and not a 'boss.'

With the last curtain call finished and the Shark Tank's lights kicked on Aza left the stage, starting to pull off the easily removable headdress, passing it to their Head Dresser that met them at the edge of the stage. Aza continued to hurry passed and headed towards Rahim, stumbling as they fumbled towards Rahim.

Rahim reached out. "You okay?" his voice boomed, grasping onto Aza with all he had, ensuring they didn't fall or get hurt. There wasn't much weight to Aza, so Rahim had to be extra careful that he didn't use too much force or he could hurt Aza.

Aza squeezed Rahim's arm. "Fine. Yes. Sorry. Distracted." Their hazel gaze reached Rahim, a flush on their cheeks and neck. "You're always there, Rahim, thank you." The moment lingered longer then needed. And the warmth of Aza's hand on his arm sent bolts of energy to every part of his body.

Rahim's body continued to pulse with excitement and worry for Aza. "Let's get you to the green room, so you can clean up and we can get you to the hotel." His heart skipped a beat.

Maybe. Aza did smile at him and they used my name. Plus, the touch.

Rahim's heart continued to jump as everyone else melted away as the two of them carried on backstage. Rahim got Aza off the stage and past craft services.

The SAP Center, or Shark Tank, as the folks in San Jose called it, was purposely built for both sporting events and music and other entertainment venues. Rahim thought the space was well thought out, and the design team, who did the most recent update, must have worked with a security professional as well, to make everything as safe as possible. Overall, this venue was one of Rahim's favorites. Especially since there were great biking trails and parks nearby, not that he got to use them often.

Next time I have some down time, I'm going to go to Alum Rock Park, take my bike and enjoy myself. If there is time.

He spared another peek at Aza, basking in their handsome features, as they moved through the space, passing different members of the stage crew, musicians, dancers, and arena security. He doubted there would be any down time, but like a potential romantic tryst with Aza, there was always hope. They continued down the hall to Aza's green room where everything was set up and waiting for them.

Chapter Three

"Did you enjoy the show?" Aza asked as the door to their changing room closed and the two were alone.

"You *are* quite the performer." Rahim answered, as the knock on the door came. He checked the door, seeing Aza's Dresser and PA. Rahim granted them access and the three began chatting about the night's performance and the issues with some of the costumes, as well as what they would need to rehearse before tomorrow night's show.

With the basics of the performance out of the way Aza started to undress, as the threesome moved to the private bathroom and shower area. Aza had a lot of parts to this last costume that would need the extra hands. Rahim stood at the door focusing on the wall as the three chatted and did what they needed to do to help get Aza out of their outfit. They left the door open a crack; however, Rahim made it a point to ignore their conversation and listen to what was happening over his earpiece with his team and Aza's security detail.

"Rahim, can you…" Aza's PA, Dee, pointed to the door he was blocking. *What? Crap. I wasn't paying attention.*

"Sorry." Rahim opened the door.

"Thanks Rahim." Ethan said with his hands full of outfits that would need to be cleaned and touched up for tomorrow night's performance.

"You sure you got this Aza?" Dee asked with a raised eyebrow. "Remember what we talked about."

"Get it done, Aza." Ethan added as he smiled up at Rahim.

"Yes. I'll be fine." Aza huffed. "You two get out of here, go and chill." They waved them off. "You have my word."

The two moved passed and Rahim closed the door after them.

"Alone… at last." Aza collapsed on the chair in front of the lighted mirror. "Ugh, I need a shower."

"I can wait outside." Rahim's graveled voice bounced around the space, as he raised a hand and rubbed his chin again, his stubble bothering him. *I should have shaved before the show, and not in the morning.*

"No." Aza said. "Plus, it's not like we have any secrets. You've seen me almost completely naked and I doubt I have anything you haven't seen before, especially being in the military." They pulled off their shoes, now only the glittery body suit Aza wore remained.

Rahim cleared his throat unsure how to answer that. Yes, he had seen plenty of naked men both in High School and the Marines, but Aza was different.

Aza stood and faced Rahim. The hazel of their eyes danced up and down Rahim's body and suit. "How long have we worked together, Big Guy?"

"Two years, this month." Rahim answered adjusting his stance, not relaxing, but moving enough to offer some relief to his feet and legs. And he rested his hands at his side.

Aza huffed, "Has it been that long?" They leaned forward, stretching, as a loud pop came from their back. "I remember it all like yesterday. I was terrified to have my home and my personal space violated in such a way." They shuddered. "Don't get me wrong. I enjoy a good wank like anyone, but…" They couldn't finish their thought as they did another stretch.

"I'm glad they caught the guy and, hopefully, they are getting him the help he needs."

"You are so much more compassionate than I am." Aza moved to their dressing table and started wiping off their face with makeup wipes. "I don't regret filing charges. I couldn't let that go; who knows what else that guy would have done. If not to me, then to someone else." Aza turned to face Rahim. "I don't care what social media had to say about the incident, I did the right thing?"

The remark sounded more like a question. So, Rahim responded. "Yes. And I'm sure he will someday be grateful."

Well if not grateful, then maybe understand what he did and why he couldn't act like that.

If Rahim was honest, he preferred Aza without all the makeup and the crazy costumes, but that was him and not Aza. The clothes and the makeup were Aza, they were a part of them. It was who they were, and Rahim wouldn't want them any other way.

"You walked into my house, standing there like superman." Aza laughed facing the mirror on the dressing table again, pulling another makeup cloth out and started scrubbing. "You're probably more what my parents wanted me to be then who I am."

"I'm sure your parents love you. Plus, you're fine the way you are."
And if they don't. Fuck'um.

"Abso-fucking-lutely. Still…" Aza turned and waved a hand at Rahim. "Look at you. I bet no one ever messed with you. I bet you were the top of the food chain in school."

Rahim shifted on his feet. This was the most they had talked in a long time, especially alone.

"Sorry, I'm not trying to say you didn't have your issues, my God, we all do. But somehow I bet you weren't picked on." Aza faced Rahim again as he continued to wipe off tonight's performance.

Rahim sighed. "After 9/11…" he trailed off.

"Oh fuck. Right." Aza shook their head. "Because of your faith. People suck." Aza turned back to the mirror, their face red either from all the rubbing or embarrassment for their comment. Rahim couldn't be sure.

Rahim remained silent as Aza continued to get cleaned up. He remembered how people treated his parents and him after the attacks. It didn't matter that they had nothing to do with what those monsters did, still they were Muslim and that was enough. That was part of the reason Rahim joined the Marines after school; even though it had been years he wanted to show people that not all Muslims were evil bastards like those men on 9/11. It helped some, but not always.

He remembered once having to jump in and save his sister, Izaz, from some bullies. Once he stepped in, it amazed him how quickly they backed down. Aza had been right, people didn't tend to mess with him.

"You know, I don't think you and I ever get to spend this kind of quality time together." Aza leaned back in the chair inhaling deeply. "What does your family think about the work you do?" Aza stood and moved over to where their pants and shirt where hanging.

"My father doesn't mind, but my mother worries. She thinks I'll get hurt." Rahim said with a tug of a smile at the ends of his lips. "My sisters are big fans, so they are always after me to get them tickets when you're in town."

"Done." Aza said. "Anytime they want. Let Dee know, and we'll give them the whole VIP experience." Aza frowned. "I should have asked sooner. I'm sorry. Include your folks too."

"You don't have to do that, I didn't mean…" Rahim closed his eyes and pinched the bridge of his nose. "And I'm not so sure my folks would enjoy your music."

Stupid. Stupid. This is why you shouldn't be talking with the client like this.

Aza laughed. "It's my pleasure, you have no idea, well actually you do, you know how many VIP engagements I've done for Dee, Ethan and the others. So, don't worry about it." They crossed to Rahim. "Do you mind?" They pointed to the zipper of the body suit they were wearing.

"Did you want me to get Ethan?" Rahim's face and neck heated.

"I think I can trust you to help me with a zipper." Aza turned their back on Rahim, waiting. "I want to jump in the shower and get the smell of performance off me before we go."

Rahim moved closer to Aza and he placed a hand on Aza's shoulder, their skin soft and warm to his touch. Aza shuddered. "Sorry. My hands are cold." Rahim said.

"Cold hands, warm heart." Aza countered. "At least according to my mom."

Rahim tugged at the zipper as it released and he was able to open the blue glitter jumpsuit to the base of Aza's lower back, noting that Aza didn't appear to be wearing anything under the sparkly garment. "There you are." As quickly as Rahim had moved over to Aza he was back to the door staring at the floor.

The sound of the jumpsuit hitting the floor echoed in the space as if a child was banging away on a cymbal.

"Oh man, that is so much better." Aza commented. "I hate that jumpsuit. I can't wear anything under it and as you can imagine it's not the most comfortable, even with the modesty padding in the front, but Ethan…"

"I can't imagine, but you look nice in it." Rahim managed to strangle out the words.

"Thank you." Aza commented as they slipped something on. "You don't have to look at the floor anymore. All my naughty bits are covered." Their laughter filled the room.

Again, Rahim's face and neck heated and there was a stirring in his groin that he wished would stop. He glanced up seeing Aza standing there, in nothing but a pair of baby blue briefs. "Well this is me. What do you think? Disappointing right?"

"Not at all." Rahim stepped forward, then remembered that was his boss and took a step back.

Aza beamed. "That is kind of you." They moved over to their pants and shirt, grabbed them and strolled to the bathroom door. "Give me five minutes. Tops."

Rahim swallowed and nodded, his hands damp. And now, thanks to seeing Aza almost completely naked, the briefs not leaving much to the imagination as it was, he really needed to adjust the unwelcomed excitement growing in his suit pants.

Aza vanished through the door and Rahim heard the shower turn on. While he waited he pulled out his phone and started checking the details for the rest of their time here in San Jose. Focusing on his job would take care of his unwelcomed and uncomfortable excitement.

For the next couple of nights they would be housed at the Signia by Hilton, formerly the Fairmont San Jose. Aza had bought out the top floor, per Rahim's suggestion, so they could have their team close, and not have to worry about security concerns on the rest of the floor. Since this hotel was where current and former Presidents stayed, the space was one of the most secure in Silicon Valley. Rahim was comfortable with all their in-house security measures. Still there were things that he preferred to handle on his own; limiting access, having his people in the hall, and ensuring that access was limited to the staff who worked there.

After reviewing the details for the hotel, he did a check in with Nancy, giving her an update on their status, letting her know they were going to be longer.

Chapter Four

Rahim wasn't sure how much time passed, but Aza appeared freshly showered and fully dressed when they returned to the main room.

Aza beamed at him. "So much better." They toweled off their short hair. "I'm glad I cut my hair, it's a lot easier to deal with." They dropped the damp towel on one of the chairs.

"I'm sure." Rahim put away his phone, noting that he probably needed to get a trim at some point. He hated having messy looking hair, especially since that was one of his favorite features about himself.

Aza moved back to their dressing table. "I'm so glad I'm performing here two more nights. I like not having to rush out, you know?"

"It makes things a lot easier for everyone." Rahim added.

"Rahim, may I ask you something? It's personal, so if you don't want to answer you don't have to."

Rahim thought a moment, he had only moments ago seen Aza all but naked and they were nervous about a question; that was silly. "If I can answer I will."

"Well, me and some of the dancers… no, just about everyone on my team really, we've never seen you with anyone or go out." Aza's voice grew soft. "What do you do for fun? Do you date? Basically, do you have a life?"

"My work doesn't allow me a lot of free time, as you know, but I don't mind." Rahim cleared his throat. He was grateful for the work and the people on his team, plus his family who he was able to help out. And it wasn't like he couldn't take time off, he could, but he enjoyed being around Aza. "When I have free time, I go riding in the mountains or out in nature."

"Horses?" Aza asked.

"Mountain Bikes."

"Ah." Aza continued to fuss at the table pulling hair product out and fixing their hair. "What else? What about dating?"

"I was engaged once, but it didn't work out."

"Oh, I'm sorry, her loss."

"His." Rahim corrected, his voice softer then he thought it should be so he repeated. "His loss."

Aza stopped and turned facing Rahim. They had moved from their hair to putting on fresh eyeliner on their right eye. "You're gay?"

"Is that a problem?" The words were a string that pulled Rahim to his full height and caused his shoulders to become even more rigid. The words calling back memories of his drill sargent yelling attention, his movements now an automatic reaction.

"No." Aza laughed. "But finding this out, it will cost me a hundred dollars. I should have known better then to bet against Dee, she called it."

"What?"

Now Aza blushed. "I'm sorry, that isn't the least bit professional. Don't be mad. We shouldn't have… and I shouldn't have… that is…" They shook their head turning and facing Rahim as they stood up. Their gaze meeting his. "I apologize."

"I assumed you knew." Rahim countered not needing the apology but appreciating one all the same. "I don't hide who I am. Just like you don't."

"Well. No. I guess not, but you aren't your average run of the mill gay man."

Rahim remained quiet, that was why he and Quint broke up. Quint wanted him to be something more. Someone different. Quint was never happy with how Rahim presented himself and how he acted. But Rahim never changed anything about himself. He was, who he was. Rahim had spent too long coming to terms with who he was, and who he loved, to be held up by Quint and some image he had in his head.

I thought Aza would be different. Clearly not. Ah well.

"I can see I've offended you." Aza reached out a hand, then dropped it back to their side, letting out a heavy exhale. "I'm sorry. Truly."

"No. Not at all." Rahim offered what he hoped to be a smile. "I'm made of tougher stuff. I'll be fine, but I had hoped of all people you wouldn't…"

"Judge." Aza shook his head. "Sadly, I'm no better then anyone else. But yes, I should know better, especially since you never once judged me."

"We're all God's children and no one can judge us but him… or her… or them. I suppose." Rahim countered rubbing his chin, the scratching sound reaching his ears, but hopefully no further.

"From your lips to God's ears." Aza made a cross sign and quickly glanced up before they returned to their seat and went back to work on their face and hair.

Their conversation ended in a hum of a hairdryer. Once their hair was to their liking, Aza spoke again. "May I ask what happened with you and your fiancé?"

"They wanted me to be something I wasn't." The words sounded harsher then he wanted them to be. "They claimed I wasn't gay enough. That I hid behind a rough exterior, trying to pass as straight. He couldn't accept that this"—he waved a hand up and down his body—"well, what you see is what you get."

"You were too butch for them." Aza laughed, holding up a lipstick tube. "My dad never thought I was butch enough. Then when I told him who I was, well that pushed him right over the edge. Up until the time of his death he continued to refer to me as *he* and *him*. He never understood and never even tried. My mom did, but…" they played with the lipstick tube in their hand.

"I think it's even harder with family." Rahim commented. "We want them to love us, all of us, and when they can't it hurts."

Aza faced him. "You get it."

"I think so." Rahim nodded. "My parents weren't in love with having a gay son, but they didn't have a choice, so I told them, if they want to be part of my life, then they have to love all of me, and who I choose to love. If they couldn't do that then I no longer needed them in my life." He exhaled deeply. "It hurt me to say those words to them, especially with all they gave up and did for me. For years we didn't speak, but in time they came around. I think I owe a lot to my sisters Izaz and Taj."

"And after two years, I now know your sisters' names." Aza shook their head. "Am I really as self-absorbed as TMZ and social media make me out to be?"

"People love you, they really do, they see all you do, and all the charities you work with, and money you give away." Rahim reassured. "You run a business, write music, perform, and do all the things that go along with the entertainment industry; you can't be expected to know every detail of those around you."

"Perhaps not, but you aren't just anyone." Aza frowned in the mirror, picking up their brush and running it through their hair.

Rahim took a step closer, unsure what more he could, and should say.

"You're my Bodyguard." Aza continued. "You ensure my safety and the safety of those around me." They shook their head putting their brush down and replacing it with a powder brush. "I should at least know you and your staff and not call you 'Big Guy' like I do the others." Aza dusted their face with a finish powder and turned around. "In all fairness, I'm lousy with names, but your name I remembered from the start. The moment I saw you, you were..." Aza stopped and their face reddened even with the makeup on. "Well you were special... at least to me."

"What makes me so special?" Rahim glanced down at himself and the dark suit he wore. He saw his calloused hands, feet that might be too small for his frame and arms that were too long for his torso. He was nothing special.

"Look at you. You're beautiful..." Aza stopped. "If you don't mind me saying. You have perfect skin, lovely rich brown eyes, strong chin, and shoulders for days. You, my dear sweet Rahim, are an Adonis."

Rahim laughed, possibly the first honest deep laugh he had in a long time. "Thank you... I think."

"You know, if I'm being honest, I love watching you watch me when I perform. I know that's silly, but knowing you're there for me, it means a lot and I don't think I could have made it through these last couple of years without that."

"You're stronger and braver then you give yourself credit for. Not many can do what you do. You put yourself out there every day. Living your life, the way you want, for the whole world to judge and see. You're fearless."

"If you say so." Aza waved off his comment. "I sing, dance, and write music that people enjoy... for now. Who knows what that will be like in five years or ten years. I would give it all up to have someone hold me, love me, the real me and not have to worry if they're only sticking around because of who I am and what I do."

"Hey BG." Nancy's voice called over his earpiece.

"What's up?" Rahim said to his mic, stopping the conversation with Aza.

"Checking in." Nancy paused. "We have everything good to go on our end. How about with you and the Nightingale?"

"Aza is still getting ready. I'll contact you when we're on our way."

"Ten-four." Nancy's voice clicked off.

"I'm holding us up." Aza moved over to their table and pulled together the last of their personal affects for the night. "I'm always doing this, I keep everyone waiting."

"It's fine."

"No, it's not." Aza slammed their hands on the table. "I'm not a princess or prince or whatever, I'm an entertainer. A lucky entertainer who has a few albums out that people listen to, that doesn't make me special." They turned. "What you do every day. Keeping us all safe, I never think about how hard you work or what all you have to give up to keep me protected. All of you. Nancy, Darius, the others, what all do they give up so I can make us late?"

"Aza, it's our job, this is what we chose to do, like you." Rahim glanced around the space not sure where to look.

"Can I take you out?" The words rushed from Aza's mouth.

"What?"

"Look Rahim, I like you." Aza's voice dropped as did their gaze. "I've always liked you. This whole ploy tonight was to get to know you. That's why Dee and Ethan rushed out of here so fast. They told me I needed to at least ask you, or they were going to do something crazy... and trust me I didn't want to find out what 'crazy' they were going to do." Aza took a deep breath. "I know someone like you would never be interested in me, but I... well... I want to learn more about you and spend some real time to get to know you. See what's on the inside."

"I..." Rahim's heart sang out as his palms dampened and his face and neck heated. Aza liked him. Big hulking, lumbering him. The idea was completely insane. How could he have been blind all this time? All those glances and peeks at each other. Two years, he wanted nothing more than to scoop Aza up and whisk them off to the bedroom and now Aza stood there facing him asking him out.

"I'm sorry. I did it again." Aza frowned taking several steps closer to Rahim. "I should have kept my mouth shut. But you have to understand. Dee and Ethan, who knows what they would have said to you, so I had to say something. Please tell me 'no' so we can get out of here and I can crawl into bed and forget any of this happened." The words continued to rush from Aza's mouth as they reached out their hand, then quickly pulled it back. "God, I'm so stupid. What am I thinking? I probably crossed every line of sexual harassment there is in the last hour and now you're standing there and... fuck... my lawyer is going to have a field day and I'm going to have to find new security. Dammit. No one will be as good as you." Another step closer and another shaky breath escaped their mouth with their words.

The space between filled with an electrical current that Rahim wanted to pull away from, but at the same time was drawn too. He was a mouth and Aza was the flame.

"You have no idea how hard this is for me." Aza whispered. "I think you would be such a sweet person to have around, not only professionally but person—"

Rahim didn't know what to say, Aza was too close to him, and the words spilling from Aza's mouth needed to be stopped and yes, Aza had crossed many professional lines tonight but so did he, especially now, as he stood there kissing Aza, their lips pressed together. It didn't take long for Aza's tongue to find his.

Wave after wave of energy burst between them. Rahim's body now ached for more.

This is insane. This is madness. What am I doing? I need to stop. I don't want to stop. Their mouth tastes so good.

More of the orange and ginger filled his senses as their continued kiss sent lightning bolts all over his body. Rahim's hands fumbled over Aza's frame. Aza's hands wasted no time finding Rahim's belt buckle and the prize that lay beneath his layers of clothes. Rahim shifted his body granting Aza easier access. This was something he had been fantasizing for since they met, that first day two years ago. Now the two of them were alone and it was going to happen, for real.

Rahim's heart pounded in his ears and he heard each gasp from Aza as Rahim managed to explore Aza's body. His hands making their way from Aza's tight butt and thin waste to their hardening dick grinding against him.

"Wait." Rahim pulled away from their kiss, and removed his hands.
I need to take control. We need to stop.

After what felt like a lifetime to Rahim, Aza stepped back and stared up at him, his breath coming out quickly between his words.

"Why…didn't you say… anything?"

Rahim stood glancing down at this beautiful person before him, all his hopes and dreams lying there. Their bodies alive wanting more. What would happen, where would this go? What would become of him? "I…well I…"

"Never mind." Aza smiled and moved forward tugging off Rahim's suit jacket and starting to unbutton his shirt, revealing his no longer crisp white tee-shirt. "Clearly you're interested. And I've definitely been more than in-terested in you." Aza pulled him closer and started to kiss Rahim again. "Now lets' get—"

"No, please." Rahim held Aza's hands and taking a lust filled breath. He couldn't remember the last time his dick was this hard. "Not like this. Not here. When we make love, I want it to mean something. I want it to matter. I don't want to just have sex with you because we both have hard ons and have hormones rushing through our aroused bodies. I want to connect with you. All of you. I want to know you. I want it to be special and have significance."

Aza stopped and glanced up at Rahim. "You. That. Why didn't you…"

Rahim took a breath, the ache in his pants protesting against his words. "I didn't think you would be interested in me. I'm just a big, dumb security jock. And you're you."

Aza laughed. "People are fucked up."

"What do you mean?"

"Here I was thinking someone like you would never want someone like me, so I didn't say anything. For two years I've said nothing." Aza took Rahim's hand the yearning, slowly leaving his cheeks and neck. "And here you are thinking the same thing about me. When are we all going to grow up and move past our insecurities and go for what we want."

"But you, or I, could have said no." The scents of orange and ginger so strong Rahim wanted to rip off Aza's clothes and share their bodies, forget the gibberish he had said about waiting. He took a deep breath and pushed his lust down and willed his dick to start to soften; not like it would listen.

Aza nodded. "Yes, that is the risk, but isn't it better to know than to pine away. Never leaving our comfort zone." They squeezed his hand. "You're willing to risk your life day in and day out on your job. You think nothing about it. Meanwhile, I risk public ridicule on the daily and yet I keep putting myself and my art out there, and I wouldn't have it any other way. Yet…"

Rahim smiled. "Yet, when it comes to this." He placed a hand on Aza's chest over their heart. "We hide and cower like children."

"Pretty much." Aza nodded, continuing to hold Rahim's hand as the other hand rested on his chest. A heavy sigh escaping their mouth. "Does this mean you'll go out with me? On a real date, somewhere nice. Anywhere you want to go. I can have Dee make reservations. There is a good steakhouse at the hotel, or there is this fondue place in Saratoga that Ethan mentioned. It's supposed to be incredible."

"Nothing would bring me more joy." Rahim released their hand and stepped back needing a break from their closeness, especially if he was going to regain some form of control over his body.

"Then perhaps, after we get to know each other, we can explore these more." Aza pointed between their crotches, their penis still erect as was Rahim's. "And from the looks of things there is plenty I'm interested in exploring."

Rahim shifted so his boner was less noticeable and leaned down to pick up his suit jacket. He covered the front of his slacks with the jacket he now held.

"Sorry. I just." Aza shook their head and manipulated their crotch so their erection wasn't as noticeable. "Well, I'm really looking forward to being with you."

"Definitely. Me too. Clearly." Rahim inhaled as the edges of his lips pulled up into a smile. He slipped on his jacket. "It'll be difficult, but I'm willing to wait, to get to know you better. I think you'll be worth it." He fussed with his shirt and tie that Aza had almost ripped off.

"Thank God." Aza inhaled and closed their eyes. "I really want to get to know you, all of you. Despite what we almost did tonight, which would be amazing and I'm not sure how I'm going to keep myself under control." Aza laughed, raking a hand through their hair. They reached out their hand again and Rahim took the offered hand and gave a squeeze. "You really have no idea how nervous I was. When I saw you off stage, knowing I had to talk to you once I was finished. Asking you tonight, well that's when I took my tumble. You have no idea how nervous you make me. Anyway, I thought I was going to land face first, and that would have sucked for everyone.

"I'd never let you fall." Rahim squeezed Aza's hand tighter.

"You know, I don't think you would." Aza glanced over at the dressing table and their makeup kit. "Come on let's get out of here. I think *things* have calmed down enough to make us acceptable for public." They chuckled. "Plus, I'm sure Ethan and Dee are around still waiting to hear and see what happened between us."

"You sure you want to tell them?"

"I'm game if you are." They smiled. "There is only one person whose opinion matters to me at the moment and he's holding my hand."

Rahim glanced down to their hands and his pulse quickened, he wondered what his team would say. They probably wouldn't care, plus it was none of their business. And if any of them objected, well that was something they would have to work on, especially since he was the boss, and he could make life difficult for them, not that he would, because that wasn't who he was. And he liked who he was. and clearly so did Aza.

Lonely in A Cupertino ADU

R.L. Merrill

I love reading the AITA posts on Reddit, but I'm also a sucker for the love stories posted there so I decided to combine the two. I have a master's in Counseling Psychology and human behavior always fascinates me. Perhaps that's what drew me to writing romance in the first place. Join me for this social media-inspired story.

The following post was found on Reddit (Maybe. It could happen).

#AITA for using questionable methods to find a date?

LonelyinCupertino

I [M26] currently reside in an ADU (Accessory Dwelling Unit for those not living in the land of perpetual housing crises) in Cupertino adjacent to my ancestral home. Okay, it's a converted garage at my grandmother's house. Whatever. The point is, I'm sick and tired of dating failures and disasters, so I took the next logical step. My grandmother's knitting circle was over the other day and I heard Mildred Garfield talking about how her son visited a "practitioner" to cure his singleness and now he's engaged to a nice girl from Manteca. My grandmother asked if "that stuff works on the gays," which Mildred swore it did, and they both urged me to give it a shot so I didn't die a bachelor. (Yes, I was participating in the knitting circle while this conversation was going on. I knit. Fuck off if you think that's weird. I also like to hang out with old ladies, even if they throw around "the gays" in every conversation.) I decided there and then that if this "practitioner" could get Mildred's creepy son laid, then it would be worth a try. (I'm not being judgy. He is creepy.) Trust me, I've tried apps, speed dating, bars, book clubs, and even goat yoga and there are literally no available gay men in my area. At least none that want to go out with a guy like me.

I went to visit the "practitioner" and they spent a lot of time burning sticks and talking about spirits...I mean no disrespect, but the whole thing seemed kinda sus to me. The "practitioner" gave me written instructions and all of the ingredients in a gift-wrapped package for $69.99, explaining that for a DIY ritual, it was a good price and that she was sure it would cure my dating ailment.

I know this may seem drastic to you, but you have no idea the sheer amount of awful experiences I've had on my quest for love in the past three years. My point is that I was willing to try anything, even a summoning circle. Which I did. And it went really wrong.

Now I'm stuck babysitting not one but two…um…beings (I can't really call them people) because, well, they're not and I don't think they ever were human at least like I know humans to be) in my ADU. They're not speaking to each other now, but when they first appeared, they got into this huge argument in some growly language I'd never heard before and then they went to opposite edges of the circle and sulked. At least that's what it looked like. Frankly, I was pretty freaked out. I tried to send them back, but I tripped over the ceremonial robe I was supposed to wear (okay, the robe wasn't in the instructions, but it seemed like a good idea at the time) and I dropped the instruction scroll into the pig blood (I know, ew) and my robe caught fire so I used the special rum I had to get from BevMo (the "practitioner" said not to use the Trader Joe's stuff I had at home) to put out the flames, but yeah, alcohol plus fire, so I stomped all over the flames and they went out. Somehow I managed to not break the salt circle surrounding the pentagram but they were, like, yelling at me and I didn't know what to do. I called the "practitioner" and they shouted, "No Refunds!" and hung up on me so I guess I'm on my own.

Am I The Asshole? I don't want to cause these two any further distress, but I don't know what to do. If anyone has any clue how to send what I guess are demons back to their realm, that'd be great, otherwise, I might have to break the salt circle thingie and let them go about their business. I have work tomorrow and if I miss again, they're going to demote me back to the receptionist desk and then I'll have to talk to people. Ew. Wait. Maybe that's part of my problem?

Bleepity Bloop

Welcome to r/AITA. Please view voting instructions, and remember to use **only one** judgement in your comment. Only upvote helpful comments, don't downvote assholes. Please keep the thread interesting. I am a bot, and this is an automatic entry.

Skepticali-

I'm not sure why "practitioner" is in quotes, but it's obvious you're messing with stuff you don't understand and you deserve whatever shit happens.

Glairvoyant-

Don't be a dick, **Skepticali**. "Practitioner" could mean a lot of things and it's better to not assume if you don't know the right answer. And **Lonely**, you're NTA for seeking help from another plane in your search for love, but YTA if you leave the demons (yes, they most likely are demons) trapped in a field with no way of meeting their needs. Your "practitioner" was irresponsible to leave you hanging like that. If you want to communicate clearly with the demons and find out their preference, you merely (REDACTED). Once you know, you can make an informed decision about how to assist them.

~**REDACT-BOT** employed to avoid the creation of interdimensional chaos.

Glairvoyant-

And fuck **REDACT-BOT**. I'm a bringer of chaos and a believer in free will and choice.

~**REDACT-BOT** This is your insult warning. Next one will be REDACTED.

JESUSTOOKTHEWHEELANDNOWIWALK

I guess we know whether you've accepted Satan as your Lord and Savior?

Glairvoyant

One does not need to be a Satanist in order to commune with spirits and/or beings from other realms. Demons are actually quite helpful if you know what you are doing, but it sounds to me as if you got what you paid for with this "practitioner." Anyone worth their salt would have offered their assistance. And love is love, demon, human, extraterrestrial, whatever.

Skepticali-

I stand by my comment. If you don't know what you're doing, you shouldn't mess with demons. And aliens boning would be epic. Anyone got any alien porn?

Babealon Five-

I'm guessing you're single Skepticali.

LonelyInCupertino

UPDATE: Thank you so much to **Glairvoyant** for the advice, which I screenshot before the **REDACT-BOT** intervened. I did what you said and they spoke to me! It was really cool. But now I have an even bigger problem. It seems like Angara (NB972) and Damzuel (?969) knew each other a thousand years ago. They met while fucking with soldiers during the Crusades I guess? Anyway, they were allies then in causing bloodshed and they were so successful at it, they were given their own army of demons and, well, long story short, they seem to have fallen in love with each other. But then Damzuel was told by one of his demonic lieutenants that Angara was planning to sabotage Damzuel's next mission which involved eating the hearts of fallen soldiers or something, and so Damzuel was angry and he found a sorceress to send Angara back to their demon realm or whatever, when actually, Angara says they were planning to request a bond thingie, some ritual where they pledged their lives and swords together for an eternity of fire? I'm not sure, they said it didn't really translate to English, nor Spanish since I explained that I spoke a little Spanish, too. That didn't seem to impress them as they allegedly speak thousands of languages and dialects, many of which have been lost to time and human ignorance, they explained.

All I know is that they both seem kinda upset and hurt and when I told them the reason I was trying this whole summoning thing in the first place, they looked at each other and…OMG you guys, it was so sad. Like, I think they've been pining for each other all this time and maybe this whole ritual wasn't about me, but it was meant to bring them together so they could mend fences? Wait, do demons have fences? I guess, they probably use barbed wire or something. How do I help them work this out and see that maybe, just maybe, they were meant to be and they could be happy again? Just because I can't seem to make this whole relationship thing work for myself, it doesn't mean I don't know what love looks like. Right now it looks like two creatures with black, leathery skin and wings with giant horns and (one has) red and (the other has) orange eyeballs who keep sneaking glances at each other, and they're both all melancholy and infinite sadness. Anyone have any ideas?

BabealonFive

One time my brother and his friends tried to do a séance but he got the directions from his ex and they ended up hexing themselves. It was hilarious, they all walked around with 24-7 boners for like three weeks before my aunt figured out how to get it to stop. Karma, dude. It's real.

DudeBro69

Put on some, like, demon porn and maybe they'll bone. You could even make some money if you record that shit.

BabealonFive

Well, now we know who is the asshole. cough cough DudeBro69

Glairvoyant

This is a serious situation. If one of them truly tried to initiate a bond with the other, their wound will never mend and they'll be in extreme pain for the rest of their existence, which is, like, forever. You have to do something to bring them together. What if you were to set up a romantic date for them? Based on your physical description, they're most likely REDACTED and so you'll want to get them REDACTED and REDACTED. I think this might be the thing that gets them to heal their rift. BTW, I think it's very sweet that you want to help them, but you should be prepared that if they do make up, their, um, makeup sex can be quite violent and disturbing so you'll want to give them privacy. Once they're, uh, finished, you can ask them what their wish is and you just might have two beings devoted to you for all time. If that's the case, use that power for good, please. Demons are a much-maligned species of supernatural creature and I hate to see them mistreated. Good luck.

LonelyinCupertino
Update

Glairvoyant, you are brilliant. I enlisted the help of my grandmother and the knitting circle and we made them a meal with the items you suggested (yeah, screw you **REDACT-BOT**, I can screenshot faster than you) and we set up a little tea party. It was adorable. At first they didn't know what to make of the dainty tea cups and the three-tiered tray of delightful creations. Then Damzuel basically dared Angara to sit down and eat, which they did, and they were smiling. I swear, you could practically see the cartoon hearts flying off of them, which was better than thinking about the ones they were ingesting with gusto. They were surprisingly neat and tidy as they ate. I knew we'd done the right thing when Angara crossed one leg over the other and ran their hoof up Damzuel's leg and Damzuel bared their teeth at them which I think was supposed to be a smile but looked terrifying. And you were right…things did get intense. I have to work extra hours this next week to save up enough to replace my grandmother's tea set, the table and chairs, and Mildred's tea cozy. It was so worth it though because after we ran in terror and sat outside listening to what sounded like a thousand murders happening simultaneously, we went back inside and they were sitting cross-legged in front of each other, knees touching, and claws intertwined. Angara was able to tell me what I needed to do to send them back to their realm, all while Damzuel was stroking their hair. It was so beautiful. I repeated the words they told me to say, and they disappeared in a puff of acrid smoke, but not before telling me they owed me an eternal debt of gratitude. That's cool, but I don't know if I want to go through all this again.

What I learned from this experience is A. Don't fuck with things you don't understand B. Love is beautiful and will find you when it's your time and C. Demons are scary-ass motherf*ckers but when they fall in love they are just as sappy as humans. Thank you for all of your suggestions, especially you, **Glairvoyant**. I never would have been able to deal with this on my own, and I never would have been able to give them the happily ever after they deserved. At least I think they deserved it. They sure waited long enough. I suppose I can wait too.

Glairvoyant

Maybe your wait is over.

LonelyinCupertino

Glairvoyant, do you knit?

Glairvoyant

I could learn.

LonelyinCupertino

Wednesdays. It's BYOY. I'm mostly there for the snacks. These ladies know how to bake.

Glairvoyant

Lonely in Cupertino I could summon up some Y. Check your DMs

DudeBro69

Aw yeah. This is the best thread yet. Demons doin' it and now **Glairvoyant** is hittin' it.

Babealon Five

DudeBro69 you are a mess.

DudeBro69

I'd like to make a mess.

Babealon Five

Where is REDACT-BOT when you need them?

This thread has been archived. New comments cannot be posted and votes cannot be cast

I love that "aw" moment in these social media posts when the person asking for advice finds their HEA. And since the theme of this anthology is "Two" why not throw a couple of demons into the mix? I've been reading a lot of monster romance lately, can't you tell? Anyhoo, I don't recommend taking supernatural matters into your own hands for the purpose of finding a mate, but if you do, don't wear a robe around an open flame, okay? Or a cape. I think it's clear they are unsafe. And never try a summoning unless you are a true "practitioner." We have enough chaos in our world right now, thank you very much. I hope this story made you smile and gave you a little hope. Thanks for reading.

Better Than One

Liz Faraim

One is the loneliest number that you'll ever do
Two can be as bad as one
It's the loneliest number since the number one

\-   Harry Nilsson

This story was written with the simple prompt of the word "two." I did plenty of pondering about the word "two," and the first thing that materialized for me was the song *One*, because of the line "… two can be as bad as one, it's the loneliest number since the number one."

From that song lyric, this story was born, and so was a Spotify playlist I put together while writing the story. Having earbuds in and music playing is part of my writing process because it helps me block out the distractions of the world and sets the mood of the story.

If you would like to listen to my "two" inspired playlist, and you have Spotify, you can check it out here: https://open.spotify.com/playlist/5ZunmYvYVtUnVhSB7IrT6b

The rhythmic piano riff of Three Dog Night's song, *One*, emphasized each bump and jostle of the train. I tried to ignore both and absorb the poem I was reading. Much to my annoyance, I had to keep reading the same line as Danny Hutton yowled in my headphones about one being the loneliest number.

Someone tapped by shoulder. Irritated, I pulled out one earbud and tentatively looked up from my book, turning to the shoulder tapper in the seat next to me. What I saw was a lady who hadn't gotten the memo about earbuds-and-book-reading being the universal signs for 'Do Not Disturb.'

"Yes?" I tried to keep my tone neutral.

She raked her fingers through her salt and pepper hair. "Two can be as bad as one." Her voice was strained, and she had an accent I couldn't quite place.

"I… uh." The volume on my music wasn't loud enough for her to have heard the song over the train noise. Yet there she was reciting a line from the song playing in my headphones.

Do I want to engage with this lady?

I leaned back a few inches and looked her over. She looked well put together–dressed as though she were headed to an office job–and didn't appear to be high or drunk. But still, as a rule, I didn't generally chat with strangers on the train. I puffed my cheeks, blowing out a sigh, and marked my spot in the thin poetry book with an old receipt.

"Two can be as bad as one, you say? I'm somewhat of a Three Dog Night fan myself. Is that your favorite song of theirs?" *Jesus, Jess. You suck at small talk.*

The woman's forehead creased, confusion on her face. "I'm not talking about *music.*" She hooked a bit of hair behind her ear and swiped at the front of her neatly pressed skirt as if to brush away crumbs that weren't there.

I did my best to push back the thoughts that she was perhaps having some mental health issues, wondering if I should just put my earbud back in and ignore her. There were still four more stops until I had to get off the train. Just long enough to have a decent conversation, but not long enough for me to be trapped if she started ranting.

"I suppose two can be as bad as one, depending on the context," I said, shifting in my seat to face her. "But, why do you say that?"

She stopped brushing off her skirt and looked at me as if she were seeing me for the first time.

"How did you know what I was thinking?" She lowered her voice to a hiss. "Get out of my head." A bit of spittle collected in the corner of her perfectly lip sticked mouth.

I sighed again. "Lady, look. *You* tapped *me* on the shoulder and started the conversation."

She squinted at me and pulled her purse into her lap as if I were going to snatch it from her. The train rattled and rocked, taking a sharp turn in the tracks. I held out my hand to her, gesturing that I wanted to shake hands.

"Hi, I'm Jess. What's your name?"

She looked at my hand but didn't take it. "I'm Gloria." Her tongue darted out, clearing away the spittle.

"Hi, Gloria."

We both lurched forward slightly as the train slowed and then came to a stop. A chime dinged, and over the loudspeaker, the driver called out the station. A sharp breeze hit me as the doors slid open.

Gloria looked around, startled, and bolted off the train with her purse held tightly against her chest, stumbling in her heels. I shook my head and cynically chastised myself for engaging with a rando on the train.

The doors slid shut, cutting off the breeze. Thankfully, no one new had gotten onto my train car so I had the seat to myself. I put my earbud back in just as the song *Two Trains* by Little Feat started up.

It wasn't a song I had ever really paid attention to. I turned up the volume a notch and listened intently to the lyrics as I watched the city slide by. It soon became clear that the two trains he was singing about were him and his friend, who were both screwing his lady. Not at the same time, I didn't think. The next line cleared it up when he added that he thought one train would be better, so I decided he was not into sharing his lady with his friend after all.

The rest of the ride was uneventful, though I wasn't able to focus back on the poetry book I was reading. I looked intently at my own reflection in the window glass, happy with the face looking back at me. Even on the crowded train I was alone, just how I liked it.

Disembarking from the train, I frowned at the watery gray sunlight filtering down. I had hoped for at least a little bit of sunshine before being locked away in my office for the day, but that wasn't in the cards. A gray cloud of discontent started to take over my mood, and I tried to push it away as I walked to work, turning up the volume on my earbuds. Eddie Money's *Two Tickets to Paradise* was playing, which helped a little.

I hated it when my days started off poorly because sometimes those low moods stuck with me for days. So focused on my own mood I nearly missed stepping over a pile of discarded food containers and a puddle of some sort of body fluid on the sidewalk.

Jesus, Jess. Get your head out of your ass.

I shook my head and made myself pay attention. Everyone else I crossed paths with seemed to acknowledge that my earbuds meant I wanted to be left alone.

The interaction with Gloria lingered in my thoughts as I got settled in at my cubicle and worked my way through the usual Tuesday morning emails. *Two Against One* queued up next on Spotify, and I pulled out my phone to check the name of the playlist I had been listening to. It seemed like classic songs about the number two was the theme. The playlist was titled something arbitrary like Rock Jamz, with no hint of the two-ness it contained.

An analyst by trade, I decided to make a list of things that came in twos to see where that led in relation to Gloria's–and Harry Nilsson's–thought about two being as bad as one.

I pulled out my favorite gel ballpoint pen and turned to a fresh page in my notepad. I stared at the bland beige fabric that covered the walls of my cubicle, tapping the pen on my lip along to the beat of Grizzly Bear's *Two Weeks.*

I clicked my pen a few times and then started writing bullet points.

- Hands
- Eyes
- Lungs
- Kidneys
- Feet
- Socks
- Shoes
- Twins

I had to stop there, as my brain ran out of ideas. The smell of coffee bloomed in the stale office air, letting me know that Darla had arrived. She was always the second person in, and the one whose first priority each day was to fire up the coffee maker.

Her ballet flats padded toward me, so I flipped back to a page of scribbled notes from the previous week and paused the playlist. As was her habit, Darla stopped by my cubicle.

"Hiya, Jess," she said, twirling an auburn curl on her index finger. "Good weekend?"

"Mm-hm." I knew she wanted more intel from me, but I was doing my best to keep good boundaries with her. "How about you?"

She beamed, clearly pleased I had asked her. "Well, I spent Saturday helping my mom around her yard. I was in bed by eight o'clock, can you believe it? I am such a lightweight." When she said the word bed, she looked me up and down, tugging a bit harder on her curl. "And then Sunday I went to Blue Rock. Got a bit of a sun burn."

She did indeed have that angry pink hue that only redheads can achieve when they are sunburnt.

"Blue Rock? I'm not familiar with it." I knew darn well where and what Blue Rock was, and had been there plenty of times myself, but I wasn't about to let her know that.

"Yeah. It's a nudist beach on the coast. If you ever want to go with me, just let me know. It's hidden, but I'd be happy to show you the way."

I pursed my lips and chose my words wisely. "Thanks, Darla. But you know I don't socialize with co-workers outside the office."

She nodded, biting her lip as she looked me up and down, crossing her ankles.

"Hey, are those new shoes?"

I peered down at my shoes, which were a highly polished pair of brown-on-brown wingtips. "They sure are."

"I really think it's brave."

"What is?"

"Well, that you walk around in the world on your own terms. Butches put a lot on the line, with their more masculine-of-center appearance. It's like you're just giving a big eff-you to all of the haters."

She started to reach a hand out, as if to brush a stray hair off my forehead, but I dipped my chin and her hand fell to her side.

"That's not what it's about for me, I just wear what makes me feel most like, well… me. And some days that means a button up shirt, slacks, and wingtips."

I tapped my pen on the notepad, half hoping a phone would ring and save me, but also wondering if she could help me with my list. I decided I had already reached out of my comfort zone by talking to Gloria on the train. *Sure, why not?*

"Darla?"

Her eyes jerked back up to my face. "Yes?"

"I'm working on a uh… project. Sort of a word association type thing. What are some things you can think of that come in pairs?"

She smiled, seemingly eager to help. "Well, let me think for a second… "

I flipped back to my list and held my pen at the ready. As she spoke, I jotted them down.

- Earrings
- Skis
- Skates
- Chopsticks
- Flip-flops
- Gloves
- Breasts
- Legs

She paused and I looked up.

"Did I name any duplicates to things you've already written down?"

"Surprisingly, no. Thanks for your help, Darla."

"Any time, Jess. Oh, I thought of another pair."

"Okay." I prepared to write it down.

"You and me. On a date?"

I did not write it down. I looked back up at Darla instead as she leaned against the entry to my cubicle.

"Thanks for your help with my project, Darla. I've got to get back to work."

I swiveled in my chair, turning to face my dual computer monitors with my back to Darla.

"Hmph. Your loss, Jess."

I nodded and pretended to work until I heard her ballet flats make their way back to the break room, followed by the rattling sound of a coffee mug being dug out of the dish drainer.

Looking at the calendar, I saw that tomorrow was 2/22/2022. *Huh.* I wasn't usually superstitious, but the sheer number of twos I had already encountered that day raised the hackles on my neck.

You're being ridiculous, Jess. We don't buy into this kind of crap. Logically, these are mere coincidences, and that is it.

I got on with my workday, which turned out to be a standard vanilla Tuesday in the cubicle farm. I did a good job of holding down office furniture for nine hours and then took the train home.

As I lay in bed trying to fall asleep, I thought again about Gloria and our conversation. Thoughts about the number two, things which come in two, and whether two was better than one had implanted themselves in my overactive brain, and my buddy insomnia was lurking.

A faint memory floated to the surface of my exhausted brain. During high school, a friend of mine who was desperate not to be gay turned to church and tried to pray the gay away. He would drag me along to bible study and youth groups, despite me being an atheist. His youth group leader led a discussion one chilly afternoon about how in marriage two become one, as written in Genesis... Or maybe it was Mark. I dug a little deeper and the words came to me:

Therefore, a man shall leave his father and his mother and hold fast to his wife, and they shall become one flesh.

In my mind, that sentence sounded like the forming of some horrible science fiction creature. So, the unfortunate image was what happened when two became one.

I chuckled at my wild thoughts and pulled a pillow over my head to help myself fall asleep. When sleep did arrive, my dreams kept me busy, running through ridiculous scenarios involving the biblical two in one marriage monsters, which to me were almost as frightening as the thought of marriage itself.

Wednesday morning, 2/22/2022, had arrived. The alarm on my iPhone blared, pulling me out of a sweaty, frantic dream. I rolled over and pressed the snooze button, then rubbed my face and watched the ceiling fan revolve slowly.

"Hello?"

A strange voice broke the silence, and I almost jumped out of my skin.

I lived alone, so there shouldn't be anyone in my apartment. My stomach clenched as my heart nearly exploded with fright. The instinct to pretend I was still asleep was strong, but I knew it wasn't a real option if there truly was someone in my home.

"Uh. Hello?" I sat up slowly, scanning my room, which was faintly lit by the beginnings of dawn. The only things I saw were the familiar silhouettes of my dresser and television.

"Huh? Hello?"

Utterly confused, I looked around again. Still not seeing an intruder, I drew in a deep breath, jumped out of bed, and flicked on the light. Nobody. I knelt on the floor and looked under the bed. Nothing there but a stray dryer sheet. I got up, scratching the back of my neck.

The person started to whimper in a childlike manner, and that was when I realized I recognized the voice.

"Gloria? Is it you?"

My whole body shuddered.

"Gloria?" I wanted to get her talking so I could pinpoint where she was.

"Y-y-yes?"

"It's Jess. We met on the train, yesterday. Remember?"

I peeked out into the hallway, which was empty. No Gloria there.

Her voice went from frightened to tight and businesslike. *"Yes. You were digging around in my thoughts."*

Her voice was nowhere and everywhere. The only way I could describe it was that she was in my head.

I scoffed. "Come out. This isn't funny."

My hand raised and swiped at my hair, as if to hook it behind my ear. But I didn't have long hair, and it wasn't me who told my hand to do it. A chill went up my spine, and I sat down heavily on the bed.

"I can't come out. I'm... I don't know how to explain it."

I rubbed my eyes and tried to wrap my brain around what was going on.

"Okay. Um, tell me what you see. That will help me figure out where you are."

"Well, I see a white dresser. Looks like something from Ikea. There are some plants on top that have vines winding their way up around the window frame. And a black flat screen TV. I can't read the brand from here."

I sat bolt upright and looked behind me. Nope, still alone. What Gloria had described was exactly what I was looking at in my own bedroom.

"Gloria. Can you get up and go find a mirror? Tell me what you see."

"Jess, I have no idea where I am or where to find a mirror."

"Jesus, Gloria. Go look around and see if you can find a bathroom."

She sighed. Before I knew what was happening, I stood up and walked tentatively out of my bedroom, down the short hallway. My hand opened the hall closet door.

"Nope."

Then I continued to the next door and walked into the bathroom.

Standing in front of the mirror I saw myself with my usual bedhead and sleep creased face. Gloria let out a long guttural groan.

The realization of what was happening was too bizarre to grasp, so my default coping mechanism of trying to make jokes and be sarcastic came out.

"It seems you are in my head and body, Gloria. So, um... welcome?"

"Please, Jess. This isn't a time to be funny."

"I don't know about you, but this is all new to me. And the first thing that's coming to my mind is... if you are in my body, where is your body?"

She heaved a big sigh and poked at my face a few times while looking in the mirror. *"This isn't new to me."*

"So, you hijack people on a regular basis?"

"Don't be silly. I didn't do it on purpose. I don't want to be here..." She poked my cheek for emphasis. *"Any more than you want me here."*

"Gee, thanks. Okay, but where is your body?"

"Your guess is as good as mine. But if its anything like the last time this happened, when we wake up tomorrow, everything should be back to normal."

"When did this happen to you last time?"

"January eleventh, 2011."

"I see. So, whenever the date has repetitive numbers, you hijack a person for the day? Sounds reasonable," I said, my voice dripping with sarcasm.

"I already told you, I don't do it on purpose."

I shrugged, at a loss for additional snarky commentary. The whole situation was... illogical and it occurred to me that sharing my brain and body with Gloria, and not knowing how to fix it, might make going about my workday difficult and confusing.

"Gloria, I am supposed to go to work today. But this is all... very strange. I'm not really sure what to do here."

"Oh, you should definitely go to work. There's no reason not to."

I sighed, accepting the situation. What else was there to do?

"Okay, in that case, I need to get ready for work. So, um, this includes taking a shower. Sorry, but you're going to have to see me naked. And then go to work with me."

"I will just shut my eyes for the naked part."

"I don't think it will work. Because those are my eyes, too, and I need to see what I am doing."

I turned on the shower and hopped in before the water had warmed up. I liked the ice-cold water first thing in the morning. It helped get my blood pumping. Gloria did not like it one bit and yelped.

"No, Jess, this won't do."

"Chill, Gloria, it will warm up in a minute." As the water warmed up, she settled down and let me get on with things.

I went through my entire morning routine with Gloria's constant commentary. I learned she didn't like cold showers. She also didn't like the type of lotion I used or the smell of my cologne. In fact, she was opposed to the fact that me, a woman, wore men's cologne at all.

I also learned she didn't like oatmeal, strawberries, or peppermint tea. Too bad. I ate my usual breakfast and headed out the door for the light rail station. Every few steps it felt like I was trying to walk under water as Gloria tried to take over my legs.

"Knock it off," I said at one point.

A man sitting on a stoop, having a cigarette, gave me a worried look. I put my head down and kept walking, biting back a comment Gloria wanted to make to him. Then it occurred to me I didn't know if other people could hear Gloria when she spoke. I backtracked to the guy on the stoop, and he looked up at me with disdain.

"Good morning," I said.

He blew cigarette smoke out through his nose in two jets and flicked his cigarette butt in an arc over the sidewalk and into the gutter.

Go ahead, Gloria. Say something.

"*Nice day, isn't it?*"

The guy didn't respond, continuing to glare at me like the weirdo I knew I was being.

Okay, I don't think people can hear you.

"*I could have told you. I know from last time I can make you speak if I want, but when it's just us talking inside, no.*"

I spun on my heel and hoofed it to the light rail station, so I didn't miss my train. Gloria stayed fairly docile until the train pulled up at the same stop she had left on the day before. I felt myself start to stand. I fought her and made myself sit. The man on the seat next to me gave me a sideways glance and scooted away a centimeter.

Where are you trying to go?

"*Sorry, this is my usual stop. Reflexes.*"

Well, you're stuck going to my boring ass job with me today. Hey Gloria, you seem pretty calm and normal.

She chuckled.

But yesterday when we met on the train you seemed really frazzled. What was going on?

"*I had just overheard some men on the train talking about what today's date was going to be... with all the twos, and it hit me that what had happened to me back in 2011 could happen again. And then you started talking about the number two to me. It was all too much.*"

I considered what she said but didn't have much to offer in return. She stayed quiet the rest of the way to the office. As I settled into my well-worn desk chair and fired up my computer she perked up.

"*You work in a nice building.*"

I looked around my ancient cubicle and down at the stained, threadbare carpet.

If you say so.

"*So, what kind of work are we going to do today?*"

WE aren't doing anything. I need you to just hang out and let me do my thing. I'm a data analyst and need to concentrate.

"*Fine. Fine. I hope I don't get in trouble. I am supposed to be at my job today, too, and I'm stuck here instead. I never miss work, so my boss won't be happy.*"

Well, let's call your boss and tell them you aren't coming in. Go ahead, pick up the phone. Just be sure to dial a nine before you dial your work number.

My hand reached out and picked up the phone receiver and dialed a number. The receiver was at my ear and the line rang a few times before a man answered.

"Krupp Bail Bonds. This is Johnny."

"Good morning, Johnny. This is Gloria."

There was a long pause as Johnny considered. "Gloria?"

"Yes. I won't be in today." My finger snaked itself into the coil of the phone cord and fidgeted with it.

"I don't know who this is but do your phone pranks somewhere else."

"No, Johnny. Please listen. This is Gloria. I won't be in today."

"You don't sound like Gloria."

"It's me. I'm just... under the weather. That's why I sound weird."

"Hmph. All right then. I'll cover your calls today. Get some rest so you can get back to work."

"Thank you. God bless."

We hung up the phone. I considered for a moment how surreal it felt to have been physically part of a conversation in which none of the words coming out of my mouth were my own.

You can speak with my mouth?

"Obviously."

"What was that about?"

I flinched, much harder than normal because Gloria flinched, too. I hadn't spoken, Gloria hadn't spoken. Was there a third person in my head?

Turning slowly, I found Darla standing in the entryway of my cubicle. It was only then I noticed the aroma of brewing coffee in the air. I had missed the telltale sign that she had arrived at the office and I wasn't alone.

My mind spun, grasping for a response.

"Howdy, Darla. How's your day starting off?"

"Fine. But seriously, what was that call about? Sounded like you were calling in sick somewhere and pretending to be someone else."

My brain didn't come up with anything brilliant to say. I put on a sheepish face. "I was calling out for my neighbor. She's too sick to do it herself and her work has strict rules about the workers not having other people call in for them. So, a little white lie to help her out."

Darla's eyes narrowed as she scrutinized my response. Then she smiled.

"Well, aren't you a sweetheart for helping out your poor neighbor."

Phew.

"See, that's what I like about you, Jess. Always helping people out, so thoughtful."

Her eyes took on the dreamy look she got around me sometimes, and I turned back to my computer.

"Thanks, Darla. I appreciate it. Sorry, I've got to get back to work."

"Suit yourself. Talk to ya later."

I pretended to start checking my email until she walked away.

"Does that young lady have a... crush on you?" Gloria sounded somewhere between disgusted and interested.

Yes. She is persistent. Now pipe down, I really need to get to work.

The day dragged on as I kept having to answer Gloria's endless questions about my job and people I had meetings with. She was super nosy and wanted to know all the office gossip. I had to stop her from walking me to the break room several times because she wanted to talk with the group who seemed to always be in there chatting.

We stopped at Zelda's pizza shop after work and I got a slice of all-meat. I sat on a bench and tried to read my book and eat in peace, but Gloria complained the entire time.

"I don't like sausage on pizza, and I don't think it's respectable to be eating on a sidewalk bench covered in graffiti on the side of the street like some tramp."

Tramp? Jesus, Gloria. Loosen up. How the heck do you live in midtown and object to all of this?

"I don't spend time on blocks like this." My hand made a swopping motion, indicating the congested, trash strewn street. *"I go to work. I go to church. I go home."*

Wait, don't you work at a bail bonds shop?

"I do."

So, don't you deal with people from all walks of life in your work? And, based on my limited knowledge of bail bonds shops, I'm guessing yours is in a run-down part of town, near the jail, the courthouse, or the bus station. Am I right?

"Yes. But I have faith in what I do. At my job I am helping those that need it, and I run a tight ship."

So, you do spend time on blocks like this. You literally work on a block like this.

This time I swooped my own hand, indicating the street.

"Okay, yes, you are right. I do spend time on blocks like this. But it's all in the line of doing God's work, helping those who need it."

I groaned, trying to wipe away the snarky thoughts that were about to cross my mind, hoping Gloria wouldn't hear them. I just wanted her out of my head. The sooner the better. I took a big bite of pizza, making sure to get as much sausage as possible, and started humming as I chewed, in an effort to drown her out. With a slightly greasy finger I turned the page in my book. She took the hint and piped down.

After I finished my dinner, I decided to walk the ten blocks home, rather than pay to ride the train. It was chilly out, but I wanted to limit how much down time I had at my apartment with Gloria still hanging around.

She kept to herself during the walk, but once I got home and settled in for the night, she perked up again.

"Are you going to date Darla? She seemed like a nice young lady."

What? No. Although who I date isn't really any of your business. And besides, it was clear to me you don't approve of same-sex relationships. So, what is this really about?

"Nothing. Was just trying to make small talk."

I shut off the lamp and settled down under the covers. *It's bedtime, Gloria. Nice knowing ya. You'll be gone in the morning, right?*

"Well... in theory, yes."

I punched at my pillow. *What does that mean? You're here for the date with all the twos in it, and then you go back to your own body, right?*

"That was how it worked last time. So, I guess so."

Good. It's been real. Maybe I will see you on the train again some time. Good night.

I pressed the button on the little remote control next to my bed and the ceiling fan turned on. Gloria grumbled about not liking to sleep with wind on her and then started running through some sort of nightly prayers. I tuned her out and fell asleep with the comforting thought that I would wake up to only one voice in my head.

My alarm blared. I reached out with a heavy arm. Instead of tapping my phone to silence the alarm, my fingers grazed what felt like a drinking glass, which promptly hit the floor with a carpeted thud. My bedroom wasn't carpeted, and I never left glasses of water on my nightstand. The realization of those facts swept through my groggy mind, and with more effort than normal, I opened my eyes.

My brain woke up immediately when I found I was not in my own bedroom. It appeared I had spent the night in the bottom bunk of a bunkbed. The wall across from me was painted an eggshell lavender. A rosary hung from the corner of a dressing table mirror.

"What the fu…"

"*Shhh. You have to be quiet.*" *Gloria's voice echoed in my head.*

Gloria? Are you fucking kidding me? Is this your room?

"*Yes. And my body.*" *She held her hands up in front of our eyes so I could see her olive toned skin, plump fingers, and painted fingernails.*

This can't be happening. You were supposed to go back to your own body and leave me back in mine.

"*Maybe, since this all happened on a date with so many twos, we get two days together?*"

I rubbed our face with our hands. Someone in the top bunk shifted and passed gas.

Who the hell is that?

"*It's my bunkmate, of course.*"

Bunkmate? Just how many people live here… wherever here is?

"*It varies. The man who owns the house is always switching out the roommates.*"

That sounds… challenging.

"*Come on, if we want a shower we have to get in right now or we will miss our time slot.*"

I sighed, surrendering to the situation. *Lead the way.*

"*Listen, I'd prefer it if you didn't look at my body while we are naked.*"

Well, you are in charge of our eyes, so don't look at yourself naked in the mirror.

She nodded and quietly picked up a small basket with hygiene products in it, glided across the carpeted room, down the hall, and into the bathroom, which was already steamy and smelled vaguely of poop. It appeared Gloria did not have the first time slot of the day in the shared restroom.

I did my best to distract myself while Gloria showered and dressed, by reciting my favorite Lewis Carroll poem, *Jabberwocky*. Though I perked back up when it was time to style her hair, which she blow-dried and hair sprayed into a perfect curvy bob.

As we stepped out of the restroom, hygiene basket in hand, we came face to face with a man who nearly bowled us over as he shoved through the door, slamming it the moment we stepped out.

"*That's Bob. He has digestive issues and often is eager for his time slot in the restroom. He is actually very nice, once he has had his turn with the toilet and fin-ishes going number two.*" Gloria looked down at the little silver watch on our wrist. "*Okay, just enough time to grab some breakfast and catch the train.*"

So, are we going to your job today?

"Of course."

Huh.

"Will you need me to call in sick for you today, the way you did for me?"

No, no. That won't be necessary. My office uses an online timekeeping platform. I just need to enter my sick time. It will email everyone on my team who needs to know.

Reflexively I reached for my cell phone in the front left pocket of my slacks. But I came up with nothing but a handful of Gloria's flowy skirt.

Oh shoot. My cell phone must be at my place, with... my body?

"Yes, I think that's how this works."

I'll have to try and remember my password and do it through your phone. You'll have to download the timekeeping app.

"I don't think I know how to do that."

I'll do it. While we are riding the train.

Gloria started preparing breakfast and packing snacks from small bins in the refrigerator and cabinets with her name stenciled on them. Similar bins labeled with other people's names sat beside hers: Bill, Bob, Rory, Gianni, and Marta.

On the way out the door, a man's voice called out to us. I felt Gloria's stomach tighten, as a sensation I associated with anxiety, rose in her chest.

"Gloria."

"Yes, Bill?"

We turned, and I flinched when I saw a man sitting in a recliner in a dark corner of the living room. The chair cushions were filthy and nearly flattened. The chair was circled with magazines and empty soda bottles.

Does he live in the chair?

"Pretty much. He owns this place."

He grunted. "You stayed in bed all day yesterday. You know the rules here. Everyone has to be out of the house between eight and five. No lazing around."

"I apologize. I was... under the weather."

"Don't let it happen again," he said, rubbing the thick stubble on his jaw with a raspy sound that made me cringe.

His preposterous rules and apparent "lazing" of his own made me furious for Gloria. I tried to speak my mind, but Gloria shoved me down and forced a smile. "Have a good day, Bill."

He grunted again and we left. Gloria hustled down the sidewalk to the light rail station. My neighborhood tended to have a bit of trash strewn around, but Gloria's sidewalk was not about to be outdone. A car had been dumped, its hood up, wheels missing, windows smashed out, and graffiti on the side panels.

Charming.

Gloria just shrugged and kept on moving, getting us to the light rail station just as the train pulled to a stop. We boarded the same car I always rode to work, and I guided us to my usual seat. It brought me a slight bit of comfort to be in my usual seat, even if I wasn't in my usual body.

I pulled out Gloria's cell phone and found that it was a very basic model. Likely the kind someone would get for free from a tent in front of the human services building. But we were able to download the timekeeping app and mark me as out sick from work.

Gloria kept patting at her skirt and pulling it down over our knees. I couldn't figure out what the deal was until I tuned back into her and realized there was a man sitting across from us, leering at her legs and whispering nasty things. I caught the tail end of what he was hissing.

"–and after that you wouldn't walk right for weeks." He sneered, slouching in his seat, and rubbing his hands together

Ugh, gross.

"It's fine. It happens all the time. Just ignore him."

Happens all the time, like with him specifically?

"No, other men do it, too. Let's just look out the window and enjoy the view. We get off at the next stop anyway."

I'd really like to say something to him.

"Please don't. I have to ride this train in this body every day. I don't want to make it worse."

I ride this car, too. Just sit next to me, and I will keep you safe.

"That's very sweet, but I don't think you fully understand what it's like. You are always covered up in slacks and dress shirts. And you can't be with me all the time to stand up for me. I choose to just ignore them, so let's just leave it at that."

Okay.

The train slowed in hitches, its doors sliding open before we had come to a full stop. We stood and walked past the lecherous man. He reached out, his fingertips grazing the hem of Gloria's skirt. When I tried to lash out at him, Gloria overrode me, and we stepped off the train.

Her office was only a few blocks away. As we approached, I saw an unhoused man napping in the doorway. I noted that she wasn't concerned or tense about him at all.

"Good morning, Joshua. Time to move along. Why don't you go on down to Loaves and Fishes and get yourself some breakfast?"

He gathered up his worn, weathered sleeping bag. "Hi, Miss Gloria. Sorry, I overslept. Yeah, I think I will. You have a nice day."

"You too," she said as she unlocked the plate glass front door. Once inside she flipped on a neon "Open" sign in the spotless front window, turned on the lights, watered the plants, and made a huge pot of coffee.

Her desk was right up front in the main lobby. It was as neat as a pin, not a single paperclip out of place. All her accessories were lavender, from the notepad to the thumbtacks on her cork board. She plugged a headset into the complicated looking desk phone and placed it on our head, adjusting the microphone in a practiced motion.

I was impressed with how seriously she took her job and how efficient she was, clearly taking pride in not only her workspace but in keeping the office running smoothly.

How long have you worked here?

"*Thirty-two years. I started right out of high school.*"

Wow. That's really impressive.

"*I guess so. I've never really thought about it. Now, listen, a lot of the phone calls I take are from people who are angry or scared, and we will talk about confidential things. So, I need you to either zone out and not listen, or promise to keep everything you hear today confidential. And if someone is being rude to me, I need you to just sit back and let me handle it my way, okay?*"

Of course, of course.

"*I think it is sweet how you were so protective of me, back there on the train and with my landlord.*"

Well, I just don't like people walking all over you. You deserve to be treated better.

"*Maybe so, but I navigate my life in a way that works best for me.*"

I understand. I will behave. So... why would people be rude or angry with you when they call?

"This is a bail bonds office, remember?"

Oh yeah. Krupp Bail Bonds. I remember from when I called in sick for you yesterday.

"Right. So, people are usually calling from jail or a family member is calling for someone who has just been arrested. People are calling us when things are bad, and not everyone is equipped to handle those things calmly."

Got it.

Gloria perked up, and I noticed the sound of a door unlocking behind us, followed by the sound of heavy footsteps in a hallway. Gloria stood us up, walked to the small break area down a short hallway, where she selected a mug that said, "Today's Mood: Nope" and poured coffee into it, mixing in some hazelnut creamer.

Balancing the full mug, she knocked on a well-worn office door that was slightly ajar.

"Good morning, Johnny. Coffee?"

"Oh, sweet baby Jesus. I am so glad you are back. Yes, coffee me." His voice was deep and thick, like that of someone who had been a heavy smoker for many decades.

Johnny's office was just as neat as Gloria's desk. Files stacked neatly in his in-box, nothing extraneous on the desktop, filing cabinets lined up along one wood paneled wall. All the office furnishings were dated and worn, but well cared for.

"So, you feeling any better?" Johnny asked as he took a sip of scorching hot coffee, nodding in approval.

"I am. Thank you for asking. I am so sorry for missing work."

"I must say, I was surprised. When was the last time you missed work? Ten years ago, at least."

"Yes, sir. Eleven years, one month, and eleven days, to be exact. Anything urgent from yesterday that needs to be on the top of my list today?"

"Yep. I sent you a recap email last night. All in all, I think I did okay covering your desk. Hopefully I didn't screw anything up for you."

"I am sure you did just fine…" Then there was ringing in our ear that made me jump.

Gloria pressed a button on the headset. "Krupp Bail Bonds, this is Gloria. How may I assist you?"

Johnny waved us off and Gloria hustled back to her desk, mentally snapping up every last detail the person, who was crying and barely audible, was sharing with her.

And so, the day went. I got a crash course in how a bail bonds office works, and the variety of crimes people committed to need bail. Gloria was an impressively hard worker, astute, organized, and professional. She took a flood of phone calls all day, switching back and forth between English and Spanish without a hitch. Nothing rattled her when she was in her cockpit.

At five o'clock, Gloria packed up, and we headed back to the light rail station.

Gloria, I'd like to ask you a question, and I want you to know I mean no offense by it. And if it is none of my business, please just say so. I will understand if you don't want to answer.

She stepped into the train, but there were no seats open, so we stood in the back and leaned against the wall.

"Go ahead and ask. If I don't want to answer, I won't."

You have worked for Johnny for a long time and seem to run that entire office. So... I would hope he pays you appropriately for that level of work. You also seem to live a very... frugal life. I guess, I'm just wondering why you live in a shared space with strangers, don't own a car, and don't have much of your own. Is Johnny not paying you fairly? If he isn't, I'd be happy to try and negotiate a higher pay for you.

"Ahh, there goes that protectiveness again. While I appreciate it, that won't be necessary. While he doesn't pay me a full office manager salary, he pays me well enough." She paused, steadying us as the train swayed and rattled. *"I send most of my money back to my family in Venezuela. And besides, I don't mind my living situation. It is humble, yes. But I like to keep things simple. I have what I need."*

I pondered what she said for the remainder of the train ride. When we got off the train, she purchased a few necessities at the neighborhood bodega and walked the rest of the way home. At 5:45 on the dot one of her housemates exited the kitchen, and Gloria stepped in. It was her turn to use the kitchen, and she quickly whipped up a heaping bowl of ramen with fresh vegetables. As soon as she sat at the kitchen table to eat, the housemate who had been in the kitchen before her stood up and cleared his dishes, shimmying past us to wash his dishes.

Wow, this place runs like clockwork.

"It has to. Bill doesn't tolerate anyone being off schedule. It messes it up for eve-ryone else. I have seen plenty of people get kicked out over the years for messing up his schedule."

I looked over our shoulder toward the dimly lit living room and spotted Bill in his recliner, surrounded by a small orbit of filth around his chair, watching. Always watching.

This place is freaking spotless, floor to ceiling, except for Bill's area.

Gloria pointed our eyes at a dry erase board on the wall. Shaky hand-writing listed names and tasks.

Is that a chore chart for you guys?

"Yes."

But... clearly, he doesn't clean up his own area. Yet holds you guys to some really strict rules and you live in fear of being kicked out.

"Yes. But I don't mind. I just live my life and try to avoid talking to him as much as I can."

Is he... does he have some sort of... diagnosis? I can't quite figure out what his deal is.

"His deal is that he is a creep and a controlling person. But, like I said, we all just avoid him and go on about our lives."

Huh. Well, it's certainly different than what I am used to, which I guess is why it seems so strict to me. But if it's what you're used to, and it works for you... it makes sense.

Gloria said a prayer and ate her ramen and vegetables. Afterward, she slid into the kitchen at her next allotted time to wash her dishes, and then on to the bathroom for her appointed time for her evening routine. At bed-time, we lay staring at the wooden slats of the upper bunk.

The air in the room was a bit stuffy, and I would have loved to turn on a fan, but already knew Gloria didn't like fans while she slept. It was funny to me how I had been sharing headspace with her for almost two days and was already aware of her likes and dislikes, as well as growing ever more protec-tive of her, despite her repeatedly telling me she could handle herself. I heaved a big sigh.

So, do you think we will wake up separately tomorrow? Like, in our own bodies?

"I think so. Last time this happened the date was January first, two thousand eleven. So, all ones and it lasted one day. This time the date was all twos, so I think this time it will last two days."

Okay, I guess that sounds like it could be right. Although this whole thing is just so... weird. I live in a world of logic and science, and this whole experience has been so outside of those boundaries.

"Good night, Jess."

Good night, Gloria.

My alarm rang with its usual tone, and when I reached my hand out to silence it, my fingers touched my phone, which was in the same place on the nightstand as it always was. The alarm stopped and I tentatively opened my eyes.

I let out a big sigh, not realizing I had been holding my breath. The ceiling fan above my bed was on and everything in my room was just as it should be.

Gloria?

"Good morning, Jess."

I had mixed feelings when she responded. On the one hand, I was disappointed we were still linked somehow, but at the same time I had grown used to sharing space with her and was glad she was still there. It was in that moment I realized how lonely my life had been before Gloria.

So, I guess we are sharing my body today? Is Johnny going to be mad because you are going to miss another day of work?

"Well, I am not sure how this is happening, but I am in my body and am at my home, yet here we are talking. So, are you in your body at your home?"

Yes. So, let me get this straight. I'm in my body at my house, and you're in your body at your house, so we can both go on about our lives, but can still have a conversation?

"I think so."

How long do you think this will last?

"I have no idea."

Can you see what I am seeing?

"No. Can you see what I am seeing? Or control my body?"

I closed my eyes and concentrated really hard, but only saw darkness and wasn't able to connect with her enough to locate her limbs and move them.

No. I think it's just our thoughts that are connected now.

"All right. I guess we will just have to figure this out as we go. I have to get into the bathroom. You know how Bill is."

I do. Have a good day, Gloria. And... don't be shy. Feel free to say hi throughout the day when you have time.

"You too, Jess."

I smiled and decided then I disagreed with Henry Nilsson. Life as one had been lonely and isolated, but a life of two, with Gloria as my co-pilot, wasn't so bad.

I do. Have a good day, Gloria. And... don't be shy. Feel free to say hi throughout the day when you have time.

"You too, Jess."

I smiled and decided then I disagreed with Henry Nilsson. Life as one had been lonely and isolated, but a life of two, with Gloria as my co-pilot, wasn't so bad.

Two

K.S. TRENTEN

Reflections are often on my mind. An image of ourselves we see in a mirror, water, or in someone else. Reflections played a major part in my first published story, Fairest. They've haunted everything I've written in one form or another. Seeing ourselves in someone else, being struck by something which is different. This particular poem tantalizes, terrorizes and soothes the narrator with this promise.

One becomes two
She finds me in the shadow of a tree
Talking to the birds, talking to the leaves
She smiles, confiding in a private whisper
She likes to talk to the birds as well.

One becomes two
She dances ahead
Springing from rock to rock
I follow with cautious shyness
Until she sees the girl in the water.

Two becomes one
She cannot look away
Captivated by her own beauty
Smiling back at her in reflection
Ready to drag her down and drown her.

One becomes two
I catch her only just in time
Pulling her away from the edge
A edge she was so close to daring
Never seeing the danger.

Why did you pull me away?
You'd think I'd parted her from a lover
Judging by the fury in her eyes
Why should I fear my own beauty?

Two becomes one
I flinch away from her touch
Not wanting to go the edge
Not wanting to see the girl with snow-white skin
Blood-red lips and sharp teeth
Always waiting within mirrors.

Two becomes one
She laughs with sweet scorn
Incapable of understanding my fear
How can you when you're constantly chasing sunbeams?
Laughing loudly without fear of who might listen?

Two becomes one
I start to run away
Hearing the echo of laughter
Years of scorn, mocking me, judging me
I don't want to hear one more voice
Better to simply talk to the birds.

One becomes two
There's an echo to my footsteps
I hear her running, trying to catch up
Her labored breath, her soft cry to wait,
It only makes me run faster.

Two becomes one
I pick up my skirts, aware I'm catching dust

I'll be scolded and laughed at later
I've tried not to listen
It's so hard to block out the voices
Telling me what I should be.
Would she listen to them?
Recoil from the true me?

One becomes two
For she's still chasing me
Perhaps the girl in the water is chasing me, too
She'll be waiting for me in the mirror
When did she become a monster?
She used to fascinate yet dissatisfy me
She was never happy with what she saw
Other people convinced me she was a danger
Why am I still listening to them?

I stop running
I turn and face my pursuer
I don't want her to be like me
I don't want to be like me
A monster consumed with shame
My darkness will consume her light
Her warm skin will become clammy
Let her see me as I am.

She seizes my face in her hands
Her eyes reflect a vision of beauty
A mirror that must be lying
Only she won't let me look away.

You are beautiful
You have always been beautiful

She whispers against my lips
Believe in me if you cannot in what you see.

There was no monster within the mirror
Just me, seeing what others saw.
It's hard to escape the torrent of words
Trying like a wave to crush me
Hers cuts through the others
Soft, sweet, yet with the sharpness of a sword
Urging me to look, to look and see
To see what she sees when she looks at me.

I gaze at the beauty reflected back
Unable to hide my wonder
She laughs softly and kisses my lips
Two becomes one.

Stag Station

Wayne Goodman

Prompts for writing sometimes come from the oddest of places (and that's what makes them so interesting!). Our local NPR affiliate hosts a program called "Bay Curious" that answers questions about unusual aspects of the San Francisco Bay Area. I heard one program about a lighthouse off the coast of San Francisco, and this story came out of my twisted imagination. This piece first appeared in my collection of short stories, *All the Right Places*.

"What exactly is a stag station?" I asked the recruiter.

"No women, no families," came the gruff reply. "You married?" he pointed a stubby, furrowed finger toward me.

"No, sir." I would have liked to have been married, but a man can't marry another man. The recent ending of my clandestine relationship had spurred me toward looking into this job as a lighthouse keeper's assistant. "It's just me."

A glassy eye gave me a fleeting inspection. "Yeah, you'll be fine," he muttered, then issued a deep and resonant cough. It sounded like he had smoked many cigarettes for many years. "How soon can you start?" he asked as he continued to scribble on some form with the stump of a well-chewed pencil.

"I'm ready immediately, sir."

"That's good. We need someone immediately." His smile unnerved me, as he hadn't shaved in a few days and he had several missing teeth. "We can't leave Platon alone for very long."

"Platon?" I echoed.

"The lighthouse keeper. Good guy, but a little strange." The recruiter waivered a flattened hand in the air near his head as he scratched behind the other ear with the little bit of pencil. "Most guys don't last more than a month with him, but I got a special feelin' 'bout you." Again, he pointed at me.

I had a special feeling about the man I recently tore myself away from. Two years of sneaking around to spend time with him tore my soul open a bit too often. The note I left behind explained exactly how I felt.

After a hard swallow, I said, "I would like to believe that I can get along with just about anybody."

A loud laugh followed by more coughing reverberated around the cramped office walls swathed in old calendars and nautical charts, exposing more of the man's gums with missing teeth. "Yeah. Let's wait a few days before makin' any more of them judgments, you hear." He handed me a piece of paper and pointed out the door. "Take this here form to the harbormaster over there."

I stood, took the paper, hoisted my kit bag over a shoulder. "Thank you, sir."

The smile reappeared on the grizzled face. "Don't be thankin' me just yet, fella."

The inside of the cavernous customshouse echoed with conversation and mechanical noises. I stepped into the harbormaster's office and presented the form.

Within an hour the small motor boat propelled a pilot, my bag and me out through the Golden Gate, passing the old Civil War fort standing guard. The cold water sprayed up on my face, tasting bitter and salty, like tears. Mist occluded the view, and I could not tell where we traveled. Every so often, a loud, low-pitched belch, like the roar of God, resonated my head. About ten minutes later, the engine slowed, and the boat approached a tiny rock in the middle of nowhere.

We pulled up to a small metal platform, and the pilot pointed wordlessly to it. Even if he had said anything, I wouldn't have been able to hear it over the crashing of the waves. I tossed my bag onto the landing and then grabbed the wet, rusty metal, pulling myself onto the miniscule island that looked more like a submarine conning tower.

When I tilted my head back, I could barely make out the shape of the lighthouse. It appeared to be tiered, like a wedding cake, rather than the tapered, traditional smooth shape. When I considered the job as a lighthouse keeper's assistant, I figured I'd be placed somewhere remote, but at least on land. This isolated, diminutive island would never have entered my imagination.

A rickety, curved stairway wound about the rock, and I slowly made my way up. Frequently I would have to pause as menacing waves lapped at the base, and I preferred not to be a casualty on my first day at the job. Again, the deafening belching noise repeated at steady intervals, even louder now that I had arrived at its source.

When I reached the platform, I saw a gray, metal door and rapped upon it. After a few seconds of waiting, I knocked again, a bit harder. It finally occurred to me that the loud noises of the sea drowned out any sounds I might be making, and I pushed the cold, iron handle down. The door opened without resistance, and I stepped into what I can only describe as a mechanical engine room. Compressors and oil-fueled generators produced loud whirring noises. There was barely enough light coming through the smoke-stained windows to make out a stairway, which I climbed.

The next level appeared more like a small apartment with a desk, books piled high on one side, a sink and sideboard across the way, and a rickety table with two spindly chairs against the curved wall.

"Hello?" I called out.

"Who the hell is there?" croaked a gruff voice from above. Footsteps on the ceiling traversed to the top of the stairs, and a shadow appeared. The person descending would be difficult to classify. Neither young nor old, not handsome or plain, neither dark nor light, not tall or short. His face had creased into a permanent scowl, and his dark-brown hair framed it in an unruly outline. He wore a gray uniform stained with dark splotches.

"Are you Platon?" I squeaked.

"Who the hell are you?" he growled.

I explained how the recruiter selected me to be the keeper's assistant. He grunted intermittently.

"Hmmmpf!" With one of his muscular arms, he motioned me to the stairs. "Come on up, Greenie."

"Greenie? But my name is –"

"Doesn't matter what your name is, you're Greenie now." He disappeared up the stairs and I followed.

Second and third thoughts began to swirl about in my head. I wanted to be away from the rest of humanity, but I wasn't sure this was the human I wanted to be trapped in a sardine can with. Then again, getting my mind off my troubles might be just what I needed.

I could see why they did not want women here. A small, cramped place surrounded by sea swells. This could have never provided the comforts of a home.

When we reached the next floor, I saw three cots and a latrine. One of the cots had disheveled sheets. A small stairway led further up.

"Choose your bunk," Platon barked.

"Will there be three of us?" I inquired.

He made a clicking noise with his cheek that sounded rather dismissive. "Nah. The other one is only for emergency visitors."

I dropped my bag on the cot furthest from the unkempt one, figuring he didn't want to be close to me either. Without warning or asking, he stepped to the primitive toilet, undid his trousers and began peeing. I wanted to look–I didn't want to look. The sound of the splashing water rankled my ears.

When he stepped away from the toilet, I waited to see if he went to the sink to wash his hands, but he did not. Instead, he went to the stairs and began to climb. Midway up, he turned and motioned me to follow.

The next level contained storage and look-out stations. A metal ladder led up to the light mechanism. Platon stood on the only space available, and I positioned myself on the ladder so that my head poked up above the flooring. With so much machinery crammed into the glass enclosure, only one person could occupy it at a time.

A giant Fresnel lens in a shiny brass frame occupied most of the room. The huge gears for turning the lens seemed imposing and dangerous. In the midst of the great, glass heart of the lighthouse sat the oil-vapor lamp, larger than anything I had ever seen before.

Through the window plates I could barely make out the shoreline of San Francisco across the water. If I wanted to get away from everyone, this seemed like the ideal place. No one could just walk up to the front door and knock.

Platon showed me the controls for the great lamp and explained how the mechanism worked. We were to ignite it one half-hour before sunset and extinguish it one half-hour after sunrise.

There would be much to do in maintaining the lighthouse. Daily inspections of equipment, weather reporting, cleaning and polishing the lens and its housing. The smoke left by the oil-vapor lamp permeated just about everything in the lighthouse.

"This job of lighthouse keeper seems monumental," I said, making an attempt at human conversation as we descended to the level with the cots.

"I ain't no keeper, Greenie," he squawked. "I'm a tender."

That seemed a rather odd statement as I sensed nothing tender about him.

The building abruptly shook, and I reached my hand to a nearby wall to steady myself. "Was that an earthquake?" I pondered out loud.

"Nah," he retorted. "Sometimes the waves hit the sides pretty hard. You'll get used to it."

He stripped out of his uniform and began washing himself at the basin. Again, I wanted to look, but I didn't want to look. Curiosity got the better of me, and when I caught a glimpse of his manhood, I shuddered a bit. The action of cleaning must have inadvertently aroused him, and I might have stared a bit longer than I should have. His distended member formed a gently curving arc that pointed downward. I had never seen one shaped such as this before! It enticed me, and I began thinking about the possibilities for something so magnificent and different.

"You hungry?" he asked, breaking me free from my momentary fantasy.

Yes, I was hungry, but perhaps not in the manner he had intended.

We walked down a level, and he opened a cupboard filled with tins. Columns and columns of preserved food stood awaiting disposition. His hand snatched a can of beans and the opening device. I watched in awe as he made quick work of the top, piercing and rotating, piercing and rotating, over and over until the metal flap rose with majesty, as if by magic.

I stepped closer and peered inside the cabinet. Salmon, sardines, beans, beans, and more beans. Several columns had accumulated layers of smoke and could not be easily read. I grabbed one of the **grimy** cans and began to wipe the film to reveal Mixed Vegetables.

"I don't eat those," he mumbled as he pointed with a beat-up spoon at the can in my hand. "You can have 'em all, far as I'm concerned." He went back to shoveling tepid beans into his maw.

My attempts at opening a can seemed to amuse him. I had never worked such a device before, and the little blade kept folding back onto the shaft before I could get very far. Finally, he set his beans down with the old spoon sticking out, walked over and took the can and opener from me.

"Like this," he demonstrated as I observed. About halfway around, he grabbed my hand and placed it on the opening device, wrapped his hand around mine and began operating it. Once we had reached the point where the lid rose, he seized the opener and handed me a rather clean-looking spoon. "See. It ain't that hard."

Actually, something of mine had gotten hard during this training session. Without thinking about it, nor wanting it, my own manhood had become aroused. Was it his touch? his smell? the unanticipated intimacy?

The spoon fell from my hand and I bent to retrieve it. Platon let a quiet laugh escape his crusty lips. "You have a lot to learn, Greenie!"

I couldn't be certain, but it did seem as though he took a gander at my backside when I stooped down. Apparently, I did have much to learn.

After chomping through the contents of his can, Platon opened the window above the sink and tossed the empty container out into the boisterous spray. Before I opened my mouth to chastise him for such appalling behavior, my logical mind suggested it might be due to the lack of space in the lighthouse. I could only imagine how quickly garbage might pile up if we did not have adequate room for it.

As I nibbled on the slimy, lukewarm chunks of vegetables, Platon kept glancing at me from time to time. His peculiar manners continued to rattle my nerves, and his not-very-surreptitious scrutiny agitated my already-uneasy stomach.

Having reached the bottom of the tin, I placed the spoon in the sink, opened the window and reluctantly tossed the can out. For a brief moment,

I felt oddly giddy, manly, suddenly empowered by my sea-fouling action. I might have even smiled.

He ascended the stairs and waved me along. At the next level Platon ordered, "Put those on," pointing at a neatly-folded uniform placed atop my cot.

I had never gotten accustomed to others looking at my unrobed body, and having to change clothing in front of this lummox stirred up all the anxiety and dread I had ever experienced. Knowing we would be spending almost all of our time together for quite a while, my logical mind realized he might be seeing me in my undergarments with some frequency. A loud, staccato blast rang out, and a foul odor followed seconds later. Such animal behavior!

I mustered up all the resolve I could. Facing away from him, I fumbled with buttons and clasps, removing my own shirt and pants. As I donned the slightly-wrinkled uniform, I could sense his eyes moving up and down the side of my body facing him.

"Let's go," he called when I had finished changing. "I want to show you the rest of the place."

He started down the stairs and I followed. On the level with the desk, he showed me the paperwork I would be dealing with. I assumed that he probably did not know how to read or write, and that left the record-keeping work to the assistant. On the wall hung a weather station, with readings for temperature, wind direction and speed, humidity, and barometric pressure. Each day I was to report the conditions on a log.

One shelf held manuals, and I had realized I had not brought any books with me. "Is there anything else to read around here other than those?" I pointed to the manuals.

Platon stepped to the table and picked up what looked like a well-thumbed Bible. "This is the only book I ever need." He dropped it with a thud. "Come on." He started down the stairs to the mechanical level.

He explained what each of the machines did. One supplied electricity for the gear mechanism, another compressed air for the horn. The extremely loud horn that wore away at my eardrums every time it blasted forth its hellish air blast. Thankfully, we only started that up when visibility conditions diminished significantly.

Next to one of the behemoth contraptions I spied a wooden trapdoor. "What's down there?" I asked nonchalantly.

"Don't ever go down there!" he shouted back, as if protecting me from some inconceivable horror. "That's just the tanks. Fuel oil and our fresh water." One of his eyes squinted slightly. "There's no need to go below this deck."

"Okay," I responded with a nervous laugh.

"Once a month, the boys from Goat Island come out and top us off." He smiled. "Sometimes it can be a real... social event ..." Platon started up the stairs. "Let's go!" he ordered, and I followed.

From the cupboard he retrieved two brown bottles. At the table, he placed one of them at the edge and pulled down, sending the crown cap flying across the room. As he handed me the bottle, he said, "I hope you like beer."

Beer? I had never tasted alcohol in my life! Beer? Where did it come from, and how much trouble would we be in if anyone found us with it?

"The water ain't that good for drinking, and this stuff"–he popped the cap off the other bottle and took a swig–"is all we have." A loud belch erupted from his gullet.

Holding the bottle in my trembling hand, I read the inscription–"Golden Gate Bottling Works"–running in an arch on one side and found an embossed image of a bear on the other. I lifted it and inhaled lightly. A few earthy bubbles tickled my nose, and I giggled without intending to.

Platon observed my activity in relative silence as he continued to suck the suds from his own bottle.

Who brought this? When? How did you get it? My mind reeled off unnecessary questions. "Are we going to get in trouble for having this?"

"Just drink it."

I positioned the opening to my cold lips and tilted back. The first splash tasted like prison. A bitter, toxic-tasting brew assaulted my mouth. If I had been alone, I would have spit it right out. My face screwed up into a contorted display of disgust as I attempted to swallow.

"You'll get used to it," came the advice from across the way.

Somehow, I sensed that would not be the last time he would use that phrase.

After he had pulled the bottle dry, he went to the window and tossed it out. Back home, I never threw glass bottles away because we could get a return deposit for them. However, out here, I imagined there might not be a place that collected illegal beer bottles.

Platon picked the old book off the table and headed up the stairs. I began to follow, and he held his hand out. "I'm going to be up there a while. Just wait for me here."

I perused the volumes on the shelf. Maintenance manuals, instruction booklets, regulations. Every so often I heard what sounded like stomping and a few grunts from above. What kind of person made those types of noises while reading a Bible?

Drinking alcohol had been illegal most of my life, and there I stood with a bottle of beer in my hand. It kind of made sense that if you were going to violate the law, this little rock in the middle of nowhere might be a good place to avoid arrest. Another attempt at sipping the bitter swill did not improve the taste, but if I wanted to avoid catching dysentery, typhoid, or cholera, I had better get used to it, as Platon had advised.

To take my mind off the situation, I gazed out the window to the west and watched the sun slowly set. Before long, the burning ball approached the waves on the horizon.

"Come on up," came the cry from above. "It's time to perform our duty."

I set the nasty bottle down and climbed up the stairs. When I reached the level with the great lamp, Platon stood on the only spot for a person. He tugged a chain from his pocket. A watch followed, and he gave it a good look, as if attempting to foretell the future.

With no action from the tender himself, hissing gas ignited, the light burst into intense brightness, nearly blinding me, and the giant lens began to rotate on its own. I raised an arm to shield my eyes.

"How did it do that?" I asked, agog. "Aren't we supposed to push some buttons or something?"

Platon grinned and let a small laugh escape his crooked mouth. "It's aut-o-matic." He pointed to a brass tube sitting above the light housing. "That there's the sun valve. It knows when the sun sets and rises. Fancy little thing."

"Then why are we even here?" seemed like a logical question.

"What if it don't work? Somebody's got to turn the light on, Greenie."

The lighthouse could function without human intervention, yet there we were. Guardians of the essential flame.

As he descended the scrawny ladder, Platon pushed me out of the way without a word. I followed him to the pantry and watched him pull another can of beans from the shelf.

"Help yourself," he mumbled.

I found a can with no label and decided to take a gamble. I fumbled with the flimsy opening device but kept at it until the lid began to rise on its own. Inside I found little sausages. They probably would have tasted better warm, but we had no stove, and I merely pulled them one-at-a-time from the can with my unblemished fingers.

While I dined, I watched the sun set below the Pacific Ocean, gently lighting it from beyond the horizon before extinguishing to near darkness. The beacon above circled monotonously, and I soon became mesmerized by its rhythm.

After gritting my teeth and disposing of the can through the window, I went to the cot where I had placed my bag earlier. The events of the day had exhausted me, and I lay down just for a moment. With nary a stray thought, I fell into a deep slumber.

I woke to ringing bells and horn blasts. Through the window I could see a small ship sitting next to our little island home.

"Hello, gorgeous!" said a voice I did not recognize from a face I had never seen before. And what a face! Rosy and fine with brilliant blue eyes. Eyes that lowered to my midsection, where an unexpected protrusion had re-mained from a latent dream, I imagined.

He wiggled his eyebrows at me. "If only I had time to help you with that, pal." A swirling whistle escaped his plump lips. "Perhaps next time we call you can help me in the pump room." The eyebrows danced once more. "My name is Chip," he announced as he approached, arm outstretched.

With little thought, I covered my embarrassment with my left hand and took his right in mine. "It's a pleasure to meet you, Chip. My name is – "

"Greenie!" he chirped. "Platon told us. Welcome aboard!" When he smiled, one side of his lips raised a bit higher than the other. "We're your support crew from Goat Island. We brought you some fresh supplies. Is there anything you might be wanting?" His stare suggested the question might be somewhat open-ended.

At that moment, I realized I had more than one immediate desire. "Yes, Chip," I managed to squeak. "Would it be possible for you to bring us some soda?"

He giggled. "We already bring you all the soda"–he winked in an obvious manner–"from the *soda shop*"–he winked twice–"we can."

"No," it took me a second to realize he had been referring to the beer as 'soda.' "I mean real soda–pop–whatever you might call it. Nehi, something like that."

"Ohhhh, soda," he mimicked with musical tones. "Sure. Sure. Next time we'll bring you some *soda*." He winked again. "Come on," he waved me toward the stairs. "You might want to give Platon a hand with the supplies.

I followed Chip down to the mechanical room. A door stood open, and through it I could see some kind of metal arm reaching out over the water. Platon stood holding a large box.

"Here," he called to me. "Take these upstairs."

He transferred the box to my arms. I turned and struggled the heavy container of canned food up to the next level.

"One more," came the gruff voice from below.

I hoisted the box up and placed it on the floor near the cupboard.

"About damn time you woke up there, Sleepin' Beauty," Platon grumbled. "Duty time starts at sunup, Lazy Bones!"

It didn't occur to me until later that I should have asked Chip for some books as well. I made a mental note to request them next time.

Another day passed without much interaction. I tried to avoid him as much as possible, mostly staring at the meteorological instruments because I could tell he didn't understand them.

Days passed, we emptied cans and bottles, then tossed them into the unforgiving sea. Eventually, I grew to tolerate the beer beverage. Platon only spoke when absolutely necessary.

One morning he announced, "Time to clean the windows." He held out a bucket and sponge to me. Must have been the assistant's job. As dangerous as it sounded, getting some fresh, salty air might have been good for me.

After filling the bucket with water and soap powder, I descended to the mechanical level and opened the door. Like a deafening cloud, the waves crashed below me, spitting up at my feet. I took my time, pressing the soft sponge around the glass panes until I could see through them.

A metal ladder led up, and I cautiously climbed holding the bucket in one hand. At the next level, the waves distressed me less. One-by-one, I removed the built-up grime from the windows. Even with the bawl of angry ocean below, I could still hear moans from above. Perhaps Platon needed some privacy so he could read from his Bible again.

The next level proved challenging, as there was no place to stand. I had to hang onto the ladder and could only reach the windows closest to it. At the top, I saw the enormous lens through the large, curved panes. As I carefully skirted the translucent turret, I observed the various parts of the assembly that operated the light apparatus.

Before I began this cleaning task, I approached it with dread, given the inherent danger of the breakers below lapping up with every tentacled wave. If the visibility decreased, the foghorn would begin, scaring the bejeebers out of me. However, once I reached the pinnacle of the lighthouse, I realized that a calmness had descended upon me, and I had found some serenity in something I had hitherto feared.

When the supply ship from Goat Island returned, Chip held a crate of soda for me. "Don't be tossing these gals out your window, Greenie. We have to take 'em back on deposit, y'know." Finally, I could have some security about not throwing things into the ocean. We stood gazing into each other's eyes for a minute or two. "You think I could put this down?" He nodded to the box in his hands.

If it were acceptable to display my affections for him, I would have walked over and kissed him full on the lips. At this stage, I still had no inclination of his inclinations. Instead, I approached him and took the crate from him, allowing our hands to rub against each other briefly. When I looked back at his face, he had a little smile, too. The wooden box almost fell from my unsteady hands. He helped me place it on the floor. I reached out to touch him just as a loud whistle sounded outside.

"Gotta go. See you next month." He turned and descended. Once again I had forgotten to ask for some books.

A month, a whole month. My only consolation would be to think of him every time I put one of those soda bottles up to my lips.

As time went by, Platon interacted with me less and less. He hardly spoke, and we both went about our chores wordlessly.

Every week, I would go outside to scour the windows, whether they needed cleaning or not. Moans above me from Platon came like clockwork in coordination with my chore.

One evening I realized only one bottle of soda remained. I had lost track of the days and hoped that the Goat Island crew, and especially Chip, would return soon.

The next day, I began my weekly window routine as always. However, the wind had become a bit violent, the waves hungry and vociferous. As I began the ascent to the second level, my mind wandered to thoughts of the tempting and effervescent Chip. This momentary distraction allowed a stray stream of water to knock me off the ladder and into the roiling waters.

As thoughts of death overwhelmed my mind, I thrashed about helplessly, shouting for assistance. If Platon had stuck to his regular pattern, this would be his Bible-reading time, and his groans of ecstasy might mute my own calls.

Again and again, the briny cacophony sloshed me about, away from the little island and back again. With every scream, water would find its way into my mouth and down my throat. Imagining my imminent drowning blocked out almost everything else. My energy had nearly depleted when I heard a shout from above.

"Over here, Greenie!" Platon had crawled out onto the metal arm and down its chains. His hand floundered in the mist attempting to capture mine. After a few futile attempts, thwarted by the menacing movements of the sea, we finally managed to grasp one another.

With heroic strength, he pulled us both up the chain until we sat on the metal arm next to one another. In many ways, it reminded me of one of those cliff-hanger movie serials, where a handsome hero rescued the defenseless heroine from the grasps of a malevolent villain at the very last moment. Perhaps, in that instant, we more resembled Tarzan and Jane, with the not-so-handsome Platon lugging me up a well-placed jungle vine.

I heaved and coughed, making attempts to rid my lungs of the bitter seawater.

"You idiot!" he charged once I had calmed down. "Come on. Back inside." He sidled along the arm and I followed. "We better get you warm."

I followed him down to the mechanical room, where the excessive heat from the generator that usually made me sweat felt welcome for once.

"Thank you," I finally managed to cough out. "I could have died out there."

"Yeah, I know," he said with a hint of remorse.

"I'd like to change into something else." I indicated my wet clothes. He nodded as I climbed up to the level with our cots.

As my head poked up through the floor, I noticed something unusual on Platon's cot. With casual interest, I peeked and recognized the beat-up, old Bible. It lay open with several pieces of paper scattered around it. Knowing he wouldn't be far behind, I quickly glanced and saw sketches of men in various stages of undress. I just about keeled over when I saw one of me bending over my cot!

So that's what he kept in his Bible! I had pretty much figured he couldn't read, but it turned out the book had been a hiding place for his sordid drawings. That explained quite a bit about that odd behavior and grunting. When

I heard steps on the stairs below, I bolted over to my own cot and began fetching some dry clothes.

He went directly to his bed and rearranged the contents, folding some of the larger pieces before returning them to the battered book. I pretended not to notice his actions.

The rest of the day passed in silence. Neither of us mentioned either incident.

Through the evening, I kept thinking of the drawing he had made of me. When could he have had time for something like that? The man had saved my life, and I pondered its meaning. Had he taken a liking to me after all? Did I feel differently about him? Platon invaded my dreams for the first time.

In the morning, the crew from Goat Island appeared. Chip had once again provided me with a fresh crate of soda bottles. "I see you've been keeping the empties for me," he said with a bit of a grin.

I wanted to tell him that every time my lips had touched each of those bottles, I thought of kissing him full on his full lips. "Thank you," I managed to stutter. "I... I... wanted to..."

Platon appeared seemingly out of nowhere. He glanced at me, then at Chip. A growly "Hmmmmph" emanated from his throat and he scampered up the stairs. My eyes followed his crumpled form as it disappeared above, and my heart turned slightly more in his direction.

"You were saying...?" Chip prompted me.

A heavy sigh drooped my shoulders. *Stag station*, I reminded myself. I knew what I wanted but wanted what I knew.

"Thank you," I managed to say. "I just wanted to ask you to bring me some reading books, Chip. See you next month."

Harlan Adams' Neck

Richard May

Almost all my stories are inspired by a visual—a photo, a dream, a person I pass on the street. "Harlan Adam's Neck" is no exception. Online, I came across a post of a photo of a 1950s movie star and was struck by his beautiful neck, something I hadn't noticed in his movies. The photo was shot from below, which emphasized the neck. Usually, the focus is on his handsome face. A story began to tell itself to me. I wrote it down as fast as I could, shared it with beta readers, and revised, revised, revised.

Out of the corner of my eye, I noticed a tall man appear beside me in front of the avocadoes. I turned my head slightly in his direction, the better to see. He had a full head of silvered dark blond hair, cut close at the sides, and left tall on the crown. His jawline looked remarkably firm. I rubbed mine reflexively. It was beginning to sag at the middle. But my inner evaluation stopped when my eyes focused on the man's neck. It was remarkably thick, with a notable but attractive protrusion of the larynx. The skin was creamy and freshly shaved. The neck more than held its own against the broad shoulders and the handsome face, which was familiar. Had I met him before in Carmel or Carmel Valley? San Francisco?

He was smiling at me now. I tried to look away, but his eyes caught me and pulled me in. Such a deep, warm, open brown. They sparkled in some imaginary sun.

"Hello," he said in a pleasant, deep voice to match the protruding larynx.

"Hello," I answered, wishing I were somewhere else.

"Found any ripe ones?" he asked. I blinked. "The avocadoes?" he explained, indicating the conical mound in front of us.

"Oh," I replied, relaxing. "I'm afraid to test any." The incline of his head asked why. "I might cause an avalanche." We laughed together and he reached in, unafraid. There was no collapse.

"You must be very good at Jenga," I remarked.

"Pick Up Stix is more my generation."

"Mine, too," I agreed.

He gave the knobby green candidate in his hand a squeeze. "Still too firm for me. I want guacamole tonight, not Thursday."

"How about this one?" I offered him the avocado I had meant to return to the pile. "It's too squishy for me."

"Squishy," he repeated with a grin, but he accepted my offering. His eyes and face brightened. "Perfect!" He looked back at the pile. "What are you making?"

"A salad."

"Oh, then take this one." He extended the avocado that would not do for guacamole until Thursday in my direction. I dropped it into my cotton bag with the Picasso print on it.

"Now, just one more," he mused. We huddled together over the choices. He handed me several for a second opinion, causing our fingers to touch frequently. Finally, we agreed. "Huzzah!" he cried and placed the winner next to its colleague in the red plastic shopping basket dangling on his forearm.

"Harlan," he said, extending his now avocado-less hand. His eyes twinkled. Did they always do that when he told people his name?

"Steven," I managed to say with only a small hesitation mid-gulp.

We shook hands. His was warm and friendly, like his eyes. We stared at one another, smiled, and waited. My hand stiffened in his grip. *No*, I told myself. *No.* Our hands dropped in mutual discord. "Well," he said, looking puzzled–or maybe angry. "Hope I see you around, Steven." I was impressed he didn't change my name to Steve. People often do.

"Goodbye, Harlan."

I watched him amble off unselfconsciously. He had a nicely syncopated walk. Immediately, my daughter Chloe was beside me, hissing into my left ear. "Dad! Do you know who that was?"

"He said his name was Harlan."

"Dad!" She seemed very exasperated for a Tuesday. "Harlan Adams! The movie star?"

I found Harlan again, next to the apples. "He has an amazing neck."

"Dad!" Chloe groaned–for the third time. I looked at Ross, my son-in-law, for support. He gave a slight shrug of his narrow shoulders and bent his head to coo at my new grandson, who was cradled across his chest.

Chloe was the result of my early experiment in heterosexuality and the only permanent good that had come of it. She was thirty-six now and a new mother. She and Ross had come to show me the baby. I had had time between the it's-a-boy call and their arrival to grow used to being a grandfather. It was something most Gay men my age couldn't say about themselves.

Matthew was a beautiful boy, all rosy and ash blond, like Chloe. He had Ross' deep blue eyes, but experience told me they might change. Would they fade to azure like mine or even lynx blue like Chloe's? If they were brown, we were in big trouble—although I wouldn't mind if they were a warm brown like Harlan Adams'.

"What else do we need?" I asked Chloe. She had organized our dinner for tonight and several more to come.

"Ross and I found everything on our list." He gave a thumbs up. "How did you do with yours?"

"Oh," I answered with a gulp. "I got the avocado." I showed her the one Harlan had given me. "Well, Harlan found it for me." Chloe and Ross gave each other a questioning look over a burbling Matthew.

"You two seem to have made quite the connection," she noted, with innuendo in every word.

"Don't get your hopes up," I said. "I've survived chance encounters before."

"Oh, Dad!" she said, with a dramatic sigh and sorrowful shake of her head. Then, her resolve returned. "Let's see that list." She snatched it from me and marshalled my son-in-law and me to select the remaining vegetables from the multi-colored produce tables.

"Great!" she declared after we had shown her the last item. "Let's check out."

I looked for Harlan on our way to the registers and behind us in the store as we left, but there was no sign of him. I felt a moment of regret but repeated my mantra of the last fifteen years, *all men are rats*. In my life, accidental meetings of the romantic kind had not had Hollywood endings.

We drove back along Carmel Valley Road to my place up Laureles Grade in their car, me in the back seat with Matthew. My house was more interior and exterior space than I needed, but I fell in love at first sight with the small building beside it. The studio, as I called it, was closer to the ocean and had huge windows on the west and south that gave the perfect light for painting.

Ross parked the Explorer in one of two available spaces in the garage. Having room for three vehicles was also surplus, but they did come in handy for guests. Not that I had that many. I helped ferry the groceries and sundry into the kitchen and headed out for the side door.

"Dad, are you painting now?"

"I thought I would." I had an idea I wanted to rough out.

"Okay. I'll text you when lunch is ready. Is rosemary chicken breast on ciabatta all right?"

"With provolone?"

"With provolone," she answered, gazing at me fondly. I thought, not for the first time, her eyes might be Ingres but her mouth was pure Mona Lisa. I thanked her and left. She was such a good daughter. I was well aware she could have sided with her mother.

At the studio, I left the green door open for fresh air. There was a lot of that in the Carmel Valley, especially up high where I was. I set up a second easel, placed a 24" by 30" canvas on it, gessoed and ready for the fruits of inspiration. I usually made a sketch first on a nice white Canson sheet, but this time I felt I had to work fast before the feeling faded. Not to mention memory. So, I took up a brush and the outline of the face began to appear, like it was there all the time, just below the surface of the canvas. Then the neck. It came out just right. I took a step back to look. Yes, that was fine for now. I wouldn't forget the rest.

I made myself switch to one of the other canvases waiting for my brushes and paint. I had promised the Monterey Museum of Art three paintings for their next fundraiser. I hadn't expected Annie to ask for more than one. When she asked for three, I was shocked but agreed. What else could I say?

"You could have said 'no'," my daughter had answered. Finlay's, my gallery in Carmel, hadn't liked the idea either.

"Three!" Linda Finlay had exclaimed. "Annie Winslow has some nerve!" Then, she glowered at me. "And you—"

"I know, Linda. I know. But they do need the money, and Annie seems to think my paintings will sell."

"Of course they'll sell. They always do. I just hope she doesn't let them go for cheap. That would devalue the rest of your work," she sniffed. "I'll call her and make sure the prices she decides on are correct."

"Shouldn't you wait until I've painted them?"

She looked at me as if to say what a novel idea. "Of course, just let me know and I'll pop by your place to take a look. And Steven," she said with a warning in her voice. "Make sure they're small."

They were, just 12" by 16". Triplets, although fraternal, not identical.

I worked diligently on all four paintings. The smaller three were my usual–landscapes of the Central Coast. The painting of Harlan was different for me. I don't think I'd done a portrait since Chloe was a teenager. I'd have to do one of the baby now or she'd be hurt. I never wanted to hurt my daughter. Never.

"Are they done?" Linda asked every other day. Finally, I could answer in the affirmative. "Great! I'll stop by tomorrow morning. Wait, Wednesday would be better for me. Threeish?"

No painting of mine was ever "done" in the strictest sense. I always saw something I could do better, but at some point I made myself stop. I didn't want to be Bonnard "fixing" his painting in a museum while a friend distracted the guard. I did understand—and sympathize with–his compulsion to add another brushstroke here and there, but–as yet–I'd never taken wet paint and white bristles to an exhibition. The three little paintings were done, or at least done enough. I resisted the urge to make adjustments before Linda arrived.

Harlan's portrait was also finished. Surprisingly, I hadn't tried to touch it up. One day, looking at it a couple paces away, I said out loud, "Stop, Steven" and I did. Harlan Adams' Neck. I almost called it that but resisted whimsy and wrote on the back in my best calligraphy, "Portrait of Harlan Adams."

Linda made quick work of the three pieces for Monterey. "Good," she said when I set them out on table easels. I wasn't sure whether she meant the size or the results. "$20,000 for each of them."

"Linda," I cautioned. "The museum has to be able to sell them."

"Okay," she harrumphed. "Three for $50,000."

"Linda, be serious."

"Oh, all right. $7,500 each—and not a penny less! Now," she said. "What else have you been working on?"

"Not much."

"What's that over there? Since when do you paint portraits?"

"It's nothing," I said. Why hadn't I put Harlan away?

"Nothing? It's gorgeous. Wait. I know this person. Oh, what's his name? The old movie actor. So beautiful in his day. Still pretty good looking, apparently. Help me here, Steven."

"Harlan Adams," I said to put an end to her clue hunting.

"That's it." She looked at the painting up close, back, left, right. She turned to me. "Is this what he looks like now?"

I gave her a look. "Of course."

"I thought maybe you were painting from old photos. Is his neck really that thick?"

"Yes."

"Hmm." She looked back at the painting. "How long have you known him?"

"I don't really."

She waited.

"We met over the avocadoes at Harvest Market."

Linda guffawed, then apologized. "I'm sorry. But you have to admit–Do you think he'd buy it?"

"It's not for sale."

"Too bad," she mused, staring at the painting, with a hand cradling her chin. "It should be."

The museum's La Mirada location on the estero was a great place for an art show. People who wanted to see and be seen could chat outside in the rose garden and leave the inside to others who actually wanted to look at art. When I delivered my three little paintings, the curator insisted on hanging them right away.

"These are terrific, Mr. Erickson! Let me show you where I want to put them." He took me into the ballroom. At least, that's what I call it. It's the room to the right of the reception desk–big, wide, and tall, with a floor of highly varnished wood. Daylight flooding through the eastern wall of windows makes it glow. Its surface looks perfect for dancing. Glide, glide, glide. There's even a piano, although I've never seen or heard anyone playing it.

"I'm thinking of hanging them on that wall." He indicated the longest wall of the room. "In the center," he added.

I looked askance at him and the wall. "My paintings aren't very big." I felt guilty now I hadn't painted larger ones, Linda be damned.

"No worries. I'll put your name in big letters right above them. Did you have any other questions?

I didn't think my comment was a question, but maybe it was. I did ask one thing though. "Will anyone be playing the piano this time?"

Gary said, "I'll make a note of that."

The *Monterey Herald* printed my official photo and color reproductions of all three of my little paintings in the Entertainment section. The paintings looked larger than life. There was no mention of a pianist.

The opening was set for a late Sunday afternoon. The day started off gloomy and grey, as so many summer days do on the coast, but by early afternoon the fog had lifted. I had planned to arrive at La Mirada early, but the baby needed a last-minute change, and then there was a debate over who would drive. Ross insisted; I insisted. Chloe finally said, "Think of a number between one and one hundred" and Ross won. She will make a great mother.

We left the baby with Esperanza, who helps me with cleaning and cooking when need be. "Teach him some Spanish," I whispered to her as we were leaving. She laughed and nodded in agreement.

At La Mirada, people in summer elegance were streaming up the entrance drive. Servers of both sexes dressed in black pants and short white jackets were pouring champagne in the courtyards. I said hello to friends and nodded at strangers as I passed through. Gary was on duty at the reception desk inside.

"I think you'll like what you see," he said, with a wink. Gary is rather cute and it's common knowledge I'm Gay but still…I had a tuxedo on.

Chloe burst out laughing when we entered the "ballroom." "Dad, your name is larger than the paintings!" That wasn't true but close enough. I heard tinkling sounds and turned, like Pavlov's dogs, to observe a lovely blonde banging away at the Oberdorfer. Maybe that's what Gary meant, not my name in a ridiculously large point size.

Annie came rushing up with two champagne glasses. She handed one to me and tried to hand the other to Chloe, who was still nursing, and then to Ross, who was driving. Each demurred. She clinked my glass and said, "Well, then. Cheers! Enjoy the show and thanks again for donating the paintings. They're marvelous!"

Ross and Linda went off in search of non-alcoholic drinks and I navigated my way through attendees discussing art, politics, and the price of gas. There was a tall, trim man staring at my paintings. People had left space around him, as if for the Pope. His head turned to meet me. Long vertical lines emerged in his tan muscular neck from his firm jawline to his baby blue shirt collar. Something in me stirred. So much flesh.

"Hello there," Harlan said. "These are really wonderful." I looked at the price tags. All three had been sold.

"Thank you for coming. Did you see the article in the Herald?"

"Yes, but your representative had already left an invitation in my mailbox. I was going to discard it, but I saw the name Steven and your photo, so…I didn't." His eyes twinkled.

"Representative?"

"Linda, was it?"

"Oh." Just then my "representative" joined us.

"Mr. Adams," she gushed. "Thank you for coming—and for buying Steven's paintings."

My eyebrows almost shot off my forehead. Linda eyeballed me nervously to her left, and her professional smile drooped in the same direction.

"They're wonderful," Harlan said. "And $30,000 is a bargain for them."

I nearly dropped my champagne. "Each?!"

Linda tried to chuckle. "Oh, Steven! Don't be silly. In total. For the three of them," she added, to make sure I understood. I understood all right. For now, what was done was done. No refunds were allowed for the fundraiser. Linda melted away.

"Thank you," I said to Harlan. "You didn't have to."

"I wanted to. They are excellent California impressionist landscapes."

"Sounds as if you know your art."

He gave a self-deprecating tish-tosh. "Not at all. I read your bio. I do have lots of paintings though. When I moved to Big Sur, I had some galleries in Carmel recommend some on approval." I was glad to hear the *on approval.* I don't respect people who buy art as décor, especially if it's mine.

Harlan was watching me with a question in his eyes on the edge of being asked. "I do have a request," he said. That made me a little wary, but I tried to smile. Art is a business after all, as Linda in Carmel and Natalie at my New York gallery so often remind me. "Would you have lunch with me?"

I was relieved. Sort of.

"Of course. I'd be glad to."

"Do you like Anton & Michel's?"

"Who doesn't?"

"What's a good day for you?"

"I'll have to consult my calendar. And my daughter."

The full wattage of Harlan's broad smile dimmed a bit. "Your daughter?"

"Yes," I replied and looked around. She and Ross were lurking nearby. "There she is, with her husband." I waved them over. "Harlan Adams, this is my daughter Chloe and her husband Ross Williams. They're visiting with my new grandson." *Let's see, I thought to myself, if Harlan Adams is interested in having lunch with a grandpa.*

Ross and Harlan said "hello" and "nice to meet you," before staring eye to eye and clamping right hands on each other, as if it were a contest of strength and not a handshake. Why do men do that? Do I do that? I hope not.

My daughter was more enthusiastic. "Mr. Adams, I love your movies!"

Harlan smiled graciously, as if that were the first time he'd ever heard those particular words. "Thank you, Ms. Williams. Very kind. Please call me Harlan."

"Oh, then you have to call me Chloe! "Embargo" is my favorite, although "Lengthy Voyage" is great, too."

Now Harlan laughed. "Are you a film historian? Mine are pretty ancient history at this point."

Chloe gave his wrist a playful slap, which horrified me. She does not get her outgoing nature from me. Or her mother, for that matter. "They are not! No, I'm just a housewife," she answered coyly.

I intervened. "She's an assistant professor at U.C. Santa Cruz on sabbatical." Most professors I know use their sabbatical to write a book. Chloe had had a baby.

Harlan looked like he wanted to say something but didn't think he should. Finally, he mugged and told Chloe, "I just asked your father out on a date. I didn't know I had accosted a straight man."

"Oh, Dad's not straight," Chloe came out with loudly enough for everyone within social distancing to hear. She raised an eyebrow at me, "A date, eh?" I looked away.

"Good," Harlan said with satisfaction. He looked at the wall. "I've bought his paintings."

Ross said, "It is for a good cause." I could see Chloe had to restrain herself from elbowing him in the ribs.

"They're beautiful," she said. That was always her opinion, even before I was famous.

"Anyway," I said. "It is for a good cause." Ross saluted me with his orange juice.

Anton & Michel's is on one of those tree-lined, flower-bedecked streets in downtown Carmel tourists don't always get to. Linda takes me there after I've delivered a new crop of paintings to her. She likes to sit at one of the outside tables facing the fountain. I prefer inside, in the bowed window space. When I arrived for my lunch with Harlan, he was seated at neither.

"Is this table all right?" he asked. It was in the interior section reserved for private parties. I looked around the otherwise empty room.

"Is anyone joining us?"

"I hope not."

I nodded at the several other tables. "Might get a little lonely in here. And," I added. "It seems a little weird. Is this where they usually seat you?"

He laughed and stood up. "Where do you want to sit?"

Our server entered, as if we'd called for her.

"Is anything wrong?"

I looked at her name tag. "Jackie, could we move to a different table?"

"Of course! Inside or outside?" I looked at Harlan, who mouthed inside.

"Inside." I answered.

She started to lead us to the bowed window, which was right in the middle of things.

"How about this one?" I asked, redirecting us to a table by the door no one used. I figured Harlan preferred out of the way.

"Fine with me," he said.

Jackie smiled. "I'll let the maître d' know. Would you like to hear the specials?" She recited them, then left us to peruse the wine list and the regular menu.

Harlan rested one hand on the table and leaned back, as if I were a painting and he needed to take a better look.

He set the menu down on the table. "Do you come here often?" he asked.

"Twice a year with Linda from my gallery."

"Your representative?"

"Did she really call herself that? Well, I guess she is. She represents me as a painter."

"She does a good job," He fiddled with his fork, then looked up in what I assumed was a telegenic signature move. His eyes sparkled again. So did his teeth. "She said you have another painting I might be interested in. A portrait of me."

I cursed Linda's salesmanship and visualized the server reappearing at that moment. It worked. "Do you gentlemen have any questions?" she asked.

I looked at my menu to hide my chagrin. "I think I'll have the lamb sliders."

Harlan answered, "The seabass special sounds good. How about some wine?" he asked me.

"Maybe a glass," I agreed. I let him pick.

I thought he'd bring up the portrait again, but instead he whispered, "Don't look now but someone is approaching from behind you."

I looked around. It wasn't an axe murderer, just a middle-aged matron in pants, an oversized sweater, and a big slouchy straw hat. She had money written all over her. Probably one of his fans. I prepared to be ignored.

The lady with the hat confronted me. "Oh, Mr. Erickson, I loved those three darling little paintings of yours at the fundraiser! I so wanted one of them, but all three were sold by the time I got there, and I was right on time, too. But I met your representative—"

"Linda?" Harlan suggested.

"Yes, Linda," she answered offhandedly, not looking at him. "She mentioned her gallery. I'm going to stop by before I go home."

"Thank you," I said. "Where is home?" I guessed Laguna Nigel.

"Palm Beach. Your painting will be a souvenir of California for me." She looked at Harlan without any apparent recognition and smiled apologetically. "Well, I'm sorry I interrupted your lunch, but I had to tell you how much I admire your work. Goodbye!" She waved. Harlan and I waved back.

I leaned toward him. "I thought sure she was one of your fans."

"Maybe her mother," he muttered. "Now, is it true…"

The server arrived with our wine, a German riesling. She showed Harlan the label, poured him a sip, and waited, bottle in one hand and the other crooked behind her back while he tasted the splash. He smiled and nodded. She filled my glass, then his.

As she vanished, we clinked glasses. "Prosit!" he said.

"Cheers!" I answered.

"Now, about that painting…" he began. I admitted to its existence. "I'd like to see it. How about I stop by?"

I couldn't very well tell him it wasn't for sale. Too many follow-up questions might ensue. And it seemed rude to say no to his stopping by. I'd set a ridiculously high price. Maybe I could say it was promised to a museum. Did the movies have one? In any case, we set to negotiating a date and time.

"How about tomorrow morning?"

I hate to disappoint people–especially, for some reason, this one but I told the truth. "I paint mornings."

"So, how about afternoon tomorrow? Five? Then I can take you to dinner."

"I'm afraid I couldn't I already have plans with my daughter and her family."

"Oh, well. Soon then. I'll stop by at four, if that's all right?"

My mind thought he was being pretty pushy but my mouth couldn't say *no*, so I just smiled and nodded, like he had at the lady from Palm Beach.

Promptly at 4 p.m. the following day, the gate intercom announced "Harlan Adams." My daughter leapt to buzz him in. "Dad! You didn't tell me!"

I thought to myself, *I was hoping he'd cancel or not show up*, but to her I said, "He wants to look at more of my paintings."

She covered a laugh and rushed out the front door. I hurried after her. Heaven knows what she'd say to him if left on her own. An expensive-looking convertible was navigating its way down the incline and around the curve to my house, which was perched on the side of a cliff. Harlan had sunglasses on, looking very much the movie star. He saw us and waved. I wanted to yell, *keep both hands on the wheel*, but restrained myself. There's a guardrail but, for some reason, I was afraid he'd drive over the edge. My heartbeat slowed as his car stopped in front of my door.

"Harlan!" Chloe yelled, waving. She rushed to the driver's side. "So glad to see you again." She opened the door for him and, without a moment's hesitation, gave him a huge Chloe hug as soon as he'd gotten out of the car. What a way to treat a celebrity.

"Thanks for coming," I said, preferring a handshake to a hug.

"Come on in the house," Chloe said and almost trotted ahead of us. Harlan smirked at me and followed her more sedately into the house. I had trouble getting my feet to move. Men did not cross my portal, unless they were the plumber or some sort of repairmen and Esperanza handled fix-it matters.

Chloe leaned out the door at me. "Dad!" she commanded, and I got my size elevens in gear. I arrived in the parlor in time to hear, "Would you like a drink, Harlan? Glass of wine? Here, Ross. Give me the baby and mix something." She leaned toward Harlan and informed him that "Ross was a terrific bartender."

"Got me through college," the terrific bartender added. "What would you like, Mr. Adams?"

"Oh, please. Harlan. Well, what are you having?" he asked me.

I wanted to answer irritably that I hadn't planned on having anything, but Chloe spoke before I could breach etiquette that badly. "What about martinis? Ross makes amazing martinis. I can't have one of course, but you three men can."

"Martinis it is then," Ross said and began pouring liquids into the cocktail shaker.

"I'll get the ice!" Chloe said, handing me the baby.

Harlan peered into the bundle in my arms. "So, this is the grandson?"

"Yes. Matthew."

"Matthew," he repeated and held out a finger. The baby latched onto it and wouldn't let go. "Strong, isn't he?"

"We hope he'll be a sumo wrestler," Chloe said as she breezed by with an ice bucket. Ross shoveled some cubes into the shaker and began vigorously mixing the drink. "Takes after his father," she said.

"That's me," Ross agreed. "Retired sumo wrestler." He poured liquid into three glasses and plopped an olive into each. "I make mine a little dirty," he said, meaning the olive juice. Harlan looked as if he were restraining himself from making a comment and, for once, Chloe did too. We took our first sips in silence but, after that, lively conversation followed. First, details about Matthew. Then, what Chloe taught and, upon learning it was English, what her favorite books were. Then they covered old movies, several of which were Harlan's. It was nearly five when I suggested Harlan and I adjourn to my studio.

He jumped up, looking chagrined. "That's right. You all have a dinner. I'm sorry for taking up so much of your time."

Chloe's face brightened and her mouth opened. *Oh no*, I thought. "Why don't you come with us? We're just going to Terry's Lounge in Carmel so nothing fancy." Harlan was dressed in a lavender short-sleeved shirt open two buttons at the neck displaying a tan and white slacks displaying muscular thighs and a tight crotch. Not fancy by any means but the outfit looked mighty good on him, I had to admit. Probably everything looked mighty good on him.

Harlan looked at me and, in spite of myself, I smiled so he, thus encouraged, agreed. "Nothing fancy is fine with me. Is there still time to look at the painting?"

Chloe's ears perked up. "What painting? Can I see it too?"

"Chloe, stay here!" I said angrily. All this activity and speed of connection was getting to me. Life on my own was quiet and slow, just like I wanted it. My daughter's face dropped. "I'm sorry, honey. I shouldn't have used that tone. I apologize. But I'd rather Harlan was able to look at it first." Chloe consoled herself with the baby, while Harlan and I left.

I held the studio door for him. As he passed by me, I appreciated that he was tall, like me.

"The light's amazing here," he said.

"I think that's why I bought the property. Anyway, here's the painting." I uncovered it and watched Harlan analyze it. Not that I had any doubts. I knew it was good.

"Is my neck really that thick?"

"You know it is. You have a beautiful neck."

Harlan moved closer to me. "You have a beautiful face." I laughed nervously. "You know you do." He leaned toward me, lips beginning to purse. I stepped back.

"This is all too fast for me. I haven't…"

"Haven't what?"

I took a deep breath. "I haven't seen anyone in years.

"I can't believe that. Men, women, and dogs must have chased after you."

I frowned. "Well, some did but I got pretty good at saying no."

"I wish you'd say yes to me." He leaned again. I held him at bay with my hands.

"I'd rather not."

His face dropped as fast as Chloe's, only he was the one who apologized. And left. I heard his car start and spin on the concrete drive. He was going to take the trip back up the hill too fast. I ran after him, then returned, covered his portrait, and took it with me. He was nearing Laureles when I opened the garage. Chloe was outside, watching.

"Dad, what happened? Didn't he like the painting?"

"Honey, I'm going after him. You and Ross go on to dinner."

"Good for you, Dad! Text me, okay?"

I put my car into gear and zoomed after my rejected suitor. *Why?* I asked myself. He's been drinking; he might not make the curves. He's…he's…. I didn't know why, and I admitted it. I just drove.

I caught up with him on the Carmel River Road. He was driving recklessly and too fast. Maybe the alcohol had gone to his head. How many drinks had he had? I figured he could see me, but he didn't slow down. If anything, he went faster. I really began to worry on Highway One. All those curves on the way south to Big Sur. I held my breath every time we rounded one, for him and for me. I wanted to slow down, but I didn't want to lose him. *I don't want to lose him*, I heard myself think.

At last, with neither of us having gone down a cliff into the ocean, Harlan slowed down and stopped in front of a wrought iron gate dissecting a length of tall metal fencing on either side. I pulled in next to him. He didn't get out, so I did—with his portrait.

"I usually do the chasing," he said to me when I arrived at his side of the convertible.

"You forgot your painting."

"I haven't paid for it."

"You don't have to. It's a gift."

He smiled, sort of. "You better come in and help me hang it then." He put the painting beside him, in the passenger seat, and hit a series of numbers on the keypad. "It only stays open 30 seconds. You better hurry." With that, he drove through, and I ran back to my car.

Harlan's house was down the cliff past a grove of eucalyptus, and so invisible from the road. There was a garage but he parked on the flat, paved space in front of it and waited for me, holding on to the painting with both hands. I pulled in next to him and we walked to a small entrance building, a separate foyer, if there is such a thing. A bridge with glass walls led us to the top floor of his house. We passed over a garden done in terraces and into a hallway. An elegant metal staircase curved down to a lower floor. We wound our way down it and landed in a great room with windows facing windward, toward the ocean, which dominated the view. Groves of cypress framed the panorama on either side.

"There's a path to the beach," he said, as if he were suggesting we go. If he was, I didn't bite.

"That must leave you breathless on the hike back up."

He smiled. "Not me. I run a lot. That's why I bought the whole hundred acres the owner wanted to sell. Well, that and the privacy."

"It gives you a little buffer from the world."

"Yes," he agreed. He studied me for a moment. "Why are you here?"

I didn't want to lose you, I repeated in my head but only said out loud, "I was worried about you."

"Why?" he asked calmly, his face bland and his eyes minus their frequent.

I looked for my answer in his face, his hair, his trim and inviting body, but most of all his neck, which I took in my hands, and gave him an unexpected kiss—unexpected at least to me.

"Well," he said with a grin, after I'd let him go. "That's a good answer. You say it's been a long time since you had anything to do with men?"

"Yes," I answered, wondering what the hell I was doing.

His eyes sparkled. "Why me then? I'm a man."

He was most definitely a man. I didn't have an answer.

"Well," he asked seductively. "What should we do next?"

"Hang the painting?"

"Hang the painting?" he repeated incredulously.

"Yes, where would you like it to go?"

He looked around the room. "Not much wall space in here. How about above the mantel?" He recovered quickly; I had to give him that. A more appropriately sized marinescape already occupied that spot. I shook my head.

"Tough audience. Okay, then. How about in my library?"

"Are you a reader?"

"I am." His eyes narrowed at me. "You don't know much about me, do you?"

"Not much," I admitted.

He nodded, as if agreeing with something I hadn't said. "Good."

"Good?"

He moved toward the circular staircase. "Yes. It's like Rita Hayworth said. 'They go to bed with Gilda and wake up with me.' In my case, they go to bed with Hank and wake up with Harlan."

I would have to ask Chloe who Hank was or maybe I could find the reference online. It would be better not to involve her any more than she already was. Meanwhile, back at Harlan's, I carefully lifted his portrait from the dining table and followed him up the staircase. Something in me stirred as I watched him navigated the stairs above me, similar to when he left me and the avocadoes. I recognized the feeling now. I hadn't had it in quite a while. Thankfully.

Harlan's library was furnished with a simple Mission-style desk in a warm walnut stain, bookcases along both sides in the same shade, and an arrangement of complementary tables, lamps, and leather armchairs in the middle of the room. The desk faced out to sea in a bay window of glass. On the left side, a telescope stood ready to scan the horizon. Or look for intruders.

"I was thinking of on the right, on an easel," he said into my contemplation of the panorama. I was thinking I'd like to paint it, cypress to cypress.

"It would obstruct the view," I said.

He sighed. "Where then?"

I scanned the interior of the room and pointed. "How about on an easel in that corner?"

He turned back to the view, then back to me. "Why don't we look at the bedroom?" he suggested with a grin. I thought to myself, *I bet that grin has graced a thousand publicity photos. I really have to watch one of his films.*

My phone buzzed. Harlan looked at my pants.

"It might be your daughter," he said.

It was. She had texted, "Is everything all right? Where are you?"

I texted back, "Helping Harlan hang a painting. Don't wait up." I deleted the second sentence and pressed send, clicked my phone to off and returned it to my pocket. Harlan led me out of his library and along the narrow hallway, past the staircase. Paintings properly spaced and individually lighted lined the inside wall. The exterior wall was more glass, showing me another side of the garden.

The progression of paintings were all representational like the marinescape downstairs but not in the same styles. The portraits and still lifes were realistic; the landscapes had softer edges.

We ran out of wall and paintings at a doorway facing due west, if my Boy Scout knowledge still held true. "After you," he said and wiggled his eyebrows. I stopped in my tracks at the threshold. "I was just kidding!" he huffed and entered the room first. Again, the outer wall was entirely glass, except for the copper-colored metal frame for the sliding glass doors. *This place must cost a fortune to heat,* I said to myself. On cue, I noticed a small fireplace on the common wall with the room next door. Two comfortable chairs, again in Mission style, were arranged near it, with a small table and lamp in between. The bed was huge. *Do they come bigger than king?* I wondered. *Emperor?*

"Well," Harlan said, with an amused look on his face.

"Sorry. I must have been daydreaming."

He looked as if he were biting his tongue.

The space above the small mantel for the bedroom-size fireplace was empty, as if he'd been saving it for his portrait. He noticed the direction of my stare.

"There's usually a painting there. It's out for reframing. Here. Let's try me up there." He took the painting from me and hoisted it onto two empty hooks. I adjusted it so it was level. We stood back to reach an opinion.

"What do you think?" he asked.

"I think…" I said, turning to answer, but I was struck dumb by the scene of him against the backdrop of the view—layers of sky, ocean, woods, and meadow. I wanted badly to kiss him again, but the proximity of the bed kept me from making that mistake. "I think it works," I said, completing my sentence.

"Great! Let's have a celebratory drink." I looked around the room and found a cabinet which could be hiding a bar. "We can have it downstairs, if you like." I felt the urge to make a flirty comment but commanded myself to *stop that.*

He was one of those people who have champagne in their refrigerator. He handed me the bottle while he opened a pale wood cabinet. The colors downstairs were lighter than the second floor, and the furniture was without hard edges, all overstuffed and comfortable.

I opened the Roderer Cristal and poured the golden liquid down the sides of the two flutes he was bending toward me. He clinked his glass with mine. "Salut!" he said jauntily. I wondered if his toast varied with the national origin of the alcohol.

We sat on the sofa facing due west, very likely just below his bedroom. "This room is made for parties," I observed.

"We should have one."

"We?"

He set his glass down. "How about you tell me why you're so gun shy when it comes to men? Or is it just me?"

I considered going home at that point but reasoned I had opened myself up for this by being there. And then there was the kiss. "It's simple really. I'm not very good at it."

"Sex?"

Was that all he was after? If so, I could screw him and be done with it. Except, it isn't always that simple. Men think one thing, sex intervenes, and they think another. "No," I replied. "Relationships. I've tried women and men, and it's always ended badly."

"How exactly badly? Yelling, throwing things?"

I smiled. He really was funny. "Sometimes."

"I'm not very good at them either," he remarked sadly. "But I do keep trying."

"There were other things I wanted to do."

"Have you done them?" he asked.

"Quite a few." And with that, I rose. "I better be going."

Harlan remained on the couch. "I wish you'd stay."

I couldn't tell him what I wanted to say, that I wanted to. I'd tried that, and like I'd told him, it never worked. I didn't have time to waste anymore. I headed for the staircase. His hand was on my arm.

"Can I call you? Or at least text?"

"I'd rather you didn't." The way I said the words was softer than the content. At least, I hoped so.

Harlan dropped his hand and said without inflection, "I'll walk you out."

Neither of us spoke again until we reached the parking area. At my car door, he embraced me with what felt like desperation. "Drive carefully," he whispered into my ear.

Along the way back to Carmel Valley, I thought of Harlan, of what I knew and what I didn't. He was famous, still handsome, and rich. Why in the world was he so desperate—and for me?

Chloe was waiting at the door. "Was hanging a painting a euphemism for something?" she asked with a laugh before she peered into my face. "Are you okay?" I wanted to say *yes* but couldn't. "Do you want to talk about it?" That I managed to say *no* to. "Would you like a drink?" I nodded yes, walked ahead of her into the family room, and collapsed onto a sofa. Why was I reacting this way? I'd said no to more than one man in fifteen years. And several women. But saying no to Harlan Adams had left me feeling depleted. Why? Because he was so needy or because I was so attracted to him? *Don't go there, Steven,* I told myself and accepted a scotch, neat, from my daughter. I wondered what toast Harlan would make for Scotch. Chloe watched me drink a moment before she settled beside me and took my hand. We sat like that, not talking, until I finished my drink.

"Thank you," I said, rising. "I think I'll go to the studio."

Chloe didn't ask why or mention how late it was. She just nodded, got up, and said she'd see me in the morning. It would be their last day with me.

In the studio, I took up a canvas, looked at the blank space, and began to paint.

August was a very productive month; I started and finished several paintings. Chloe thought I should take a break. For once, I agreed with her. I decided to take a trip and so booked passage on flights to New York and Paris, the first to visit Natalie and the New York gallery and the second to soak up some culture and autumnal Parisian beauty. A French friend said I could stay with him. He owned a narrow five-story building in the Marais. He said he had a floor I could use as a studio, but I told him I was taking a vacation from painting.

"Not a long one, I hope," he emailed back. I didn't respond.

Chloe and her family scheduled time to drive down from Santa Cruz to say bon voyage. "I'll cook dinner," I promised. I had decided on a Mexican feast, which was why I was back at Harvest Market, looking for squishable avocadoes. I'd invited Linda too, to make it an even number and not hurt her feelings. She could guess I was going to see Natalie.

I felt someone beside me in the produce section. I knew who it was. I looked anyway. I had missed that beautiful neck.

"Hello," he said tentatively.

"Hello, Harlan."

"What are you making?" he asked.

I was surprised at this conversational turn but was glad we could chat as friends. Or at least acquaintances.

"Guacamole," I answered. "What about you?

"A salad." He picked up one, then two avocadoes without coming to a conclusion.

Try, a voice inside me said.

"I'm cooking dinner for my daughter and her family. And Linda Finlay."

"Your representative," he said and tried to smile.

"Yes."

I thought a moment. *Try*, the voice repeated.

"Would you like to come?

"To dinner?" he asked. I nodded. "At your house?" I nodded again.

It sounds immodest to say but I've never seen joy spread so fast across a person's face. Sparkle returned to his eyes, which was all well and good, but when he raised his head and straightened his shoulders, my God, his neck… *You have a fetish*, I told myself. *I don't care*, I answered.

"Steven," he was saying. "Steven?" He had an avocado in hand. "How about this one?"

I squeezed it. "I'll need three. I mean, if you're coming."

His warm eyes examined me for some time before he smiled and answered, "Oh, I'll be there. What can I bring?"

"Just you. That'll be fine." *And*, I thought to myself, *that it will.*

I didn't tell him about Paris. My tickets were refundable after all. He handed me another avocado. I took it and thought, *Maybe things will work out this time.* I began to hope.

Dear Beloved Comrade

Gar McVey-Russell

My fascination with North Korea dates back 40-odd years to my shortwave radio days. I used to listen to Radio Pyongyang, as it was then known. What a strange, closed off world, one shrouded in myth as well as mystery. The broadcasts mostly focused on the glories and philosophies of the country's founder, their Great Leader Kim Il-sung. Everything revolved around him. Dissension meant death. His autocratic rule, maintained by his successors Kim Jong-il (son) and Kim Jong-un (grandson), had no tolerance for homosexuality. What would it be like to grow up gay in such a society? "Dear Beloved Comrade" is my answer to this question.

His uniform and the strong sense of purpose with which he came at me caused an instinctual reaction. I no longer roamed freely around an open market in small-town Malaysia. I was back home in South Central, a frightened nappy-headed kid who knew he hadn't done anything wrong, but felt a need to flee anyway. The big kids taught me that fear. They said, don't argue, just run, so that's what I did. I ran. The cop ran after me. I hid. The cop never found me. He gave up his search and went away. His abandoned search only proved in my mind that the whole enterprise was bullshit. If I really had done something, then he would have called for reinforcements or set up a dragnet. I slinked home once I heard the cop car drive off. It pulled away in a hurry, probably in pursuit of another scared nappy-headed kid who had done nothing.

I told my mother what happened. She didn't like that I ran. You don't run from the police, she said, it makes you look guilty. As she lectured me, I noticed that her face failed to sync with her words. The words said don't run, while her face said *do what you have to do to protect yourself*. So that's the message that really stuck.

Running here, however, had greater consequences than it did that day in South Central. This land was not my land; I am a guest here. Come what may, I had to obey. However, as he got closer, I saw that he wore an official outfit, but not one belonging to the Malaysian police. And the man himself looked foreign, as did I.

He stopped right in front of me, panting. Yes, definitely not Malaysian. I waited. He waited. Did he expect me to say something?

"You were whistling," he said.

I tried not to smirk, but it was hard. You came rushing up to me to tell me that I was whistling? The gum-chewing offense from Singapore in the 90s came to mind, but this was not Singapore and I wasn't chewing gum.

More silence. Though it had been a good minute since he stopped running, he still panted. He did not look out of shape. In fact he looked quite trim. So why the panting?

"Yes?" I finally said.

"That tune. I heard you whistling a special tune."

Truth be told, I had no idea what he was talking about. When he came rushing up to me, my mind concentrated on mangos displayed on the table that stood between us and on the lassis I hoped to make from them. Without thinking my face lapsed into a "huh?" It took him aback. I tried softening my expression. I'm a big, 6'1" black dude, a fact I'm always aware of. While working overseas, I've learned to mellow my expressions so that folks don't get hyped up around me. I call it my puppy-dog look. Earnestness eases many tensions.

"It's just," he started to say.

"Yes?"

"It's just that I've never heard a foreigner whistle that tune before."

"What tune is this?"

"When you were over by there," he said, "by the melons."

I wanted him to tell me the name of the tune, since he obviously recognized it, but he wouldn't. I always have some ditty in my head. They fly in like a passing bumblebee, fluttering harmlessly in the space, before retreating again. Seeing the melons made me think how much I missed watermelon, so maybe I had "Watermelon Man" buzzing inside me. But that didn't seem right.

Then I took a good look at him. He wore a greenish-brown suit with smart buttons trimmed on his shoulder and down the front. He wore a little cap with an insignia that at first I could not recognize, it was so small. But upon closer examination, the depiction began to look very familiar. Then I looked at his face. Yes. Korean. He was Korean. And he was front *that* Korea. I listened to Voice of Korea on shortwave that morning. At the start of their broadcasts, they play the national anthem. That must have been the bumble-bee buzzing through my head while looking at the melons. I didn't even realize.

I explained my predilection for shortwave and history of listening to North Korea. His eyes grew wide.

"I'm not supposed to listen to it," he said. "I do not know what they broadcast."

His face transformed from intense to apologetic. The panting ceased. Where before his body language communicated firm determination, it now displayed retreat. He wanted to chastise me for whistling a sacred tune, for offending Dear Leader, or whatever appellation they've applied to the new, younger Kim leading the country now. But all that bluster vanished.

"I just like the tune," I said, somewhat sheepishly. I went full-on puppy-dog now, trying to soften my large frame to appear less of a threat.

"I've never heard a foreigner who knew it," he said.

"You know the New York Philharmonic played it when they visited Pyongyang a few years ago."

His eyes grew big again. He did not know. How was it that I knew more about his country than he did?

"Are you here long in Malaysia?" I asked.

"Just another week or so. How about you?"

I was part of a trade group. Meetings. Banquets. Official tours. Logistics. Tedious at times, but interesting. I liked my down time when I get to explore the backwaters that they don't show on the official tours. I had been in Malaysia for a while, but my home base was Hong Kong.

I squeezed mangos with my hands as we chatted. He stared at them doing this. I could see his breathing changed again. Now I saw why he rushed me. Indignation has no greater fuel then forbidden attraction.

"I plan to make some mango lassis," I said. "Do you want to try some?"

He surprised me by saying, "Yes, I'd like that very much."

He liked to be called J, so even his name remained a mystery. We had dinner together a few times. We saw a movie together. I asked teasingly if these things were outside the bounds of tolerance from his government. He only smiled.

I actually referenced his peculiar homeland very infrequently. It sat in the room with us, came to dinner and the movies with us, though it remained unobtrusive. It draped itself over J like a cape, something that caught the eye on first viewing, but then regressed to the background. Though we rarely discussed North Korea, I felt that he had much pride for his homeland. I would expect such an attitude from someone of his standing. He held a rare privilege among his people: the ability to travel overseas. Many North Koreans never get a chance to see their own capital, Pyongyang, much less travel abroad. Only the most trusted, loyal comrades received that blessing, no doubt.

We spent a good deal of time at my place. He liked the homemade mango lassis. He liked the music I played. He liked looking at the setting sun from my balcony. He never spent the night, but we held each other comfortably. We never actually "did it," but that never bothered me. I respected whatever limits he felt comfortable with. I knew folks back home who kept to themselves so much, fearful of where their sexuality might take them, that they lived like cloistered monks or nuns. J had a better excuse, given his origins. Even if he felt comfortable within himself, how hard was it for him to find someone to hold, to drink lassis with while watching the sunset? For me this was a pleasant interlude with a very handsome man. For him, I hope I provided a rare oasis.

He asked me about my growing up in Los Angeles, whether I was allowed in Hollywood and if I had ever seen the Watts Towers. I laughed. Time outside the homeland has given him a glimpse of the world. He understood about the restrictions placed on black folks, the shadow we find ourselves living under. I told him that I had no trouble going to Hollywood and how I practically lived there and all the dive bars I used to visit. I could tell that excited him, the thought of a place filled with men seeking other men. I also told him how my mother took me to see the Watts Towers when I was a boy.

He asked about my mother, and I admitted that she was a difficult subject. We had a falling out after my coming out. She ranted about how she failed me, how it was all her fault. She lamented not sticking it out with my father. I didn't need a man in life that badly, I said angrily. My father was a motherfucker; the less said about him the better. She got cross and didn't speak to me for nearly a year. When we started to communicate again, we danced all around the subject of my sexuality, my dating and heartaches over this dude or that dude. I felt like Eliza Doolittle: stick to empty "how do you do" questions and the weather. That type of detachment from her and others of my family–cousins, aunts, and uncles; I'm an only child–was what helped to propel me from the US in the first place. It wasn't just the racism, I told J. I've lived overseas ever since, from Sydney to Singapore to Hong Kong.

My days with J were all too brief, too fleeting. During our last meetings, we had graduated to passionate kissing. By the time his taste filled my mouth, but before I could go back for seconds, he was gone. Duty called. The privilege of living and working outside the motherland meant obeying a strict schedule. He had to go home.

I wondered if he ever considered defection and startled myself with the thought, wondering if my attraction to him was more than I realized. Possibly. Maybe part of me just didn't like thinking of him going back to a place where he could not find the type of love he wanted or needed. He looked at me and read either my face or my mind. My mother is back home, he said, and she doesn't do well when I'm not around.

That was the first time he mentioned anything about his family. I asked how close he was to her and his other relatives. She worries about me, he said. She wanted him to find a good wife and settle down. He giggled, though melancholy darkened the dimples I liked so much. He said she worried about what will happen to him when she passes on. I asked about his father, then regretted it from the facial expression he made. I would describe J's face as neutral beauty, no forced smiles or hardened looks, but a natural gaze of lingering contentment. He banished that when I mentioned his father. My father was a motherfucker, too, he said. Hearing that word come from his mouth shocked me. It also kinda turned me on.

But then his next words really threw me for a loop. You should come visit Pyongyang, he said. J thought that he would be assigned tour guide duties for a while, to stay home. That way he could take care of his mother more easily. I laughed. Seriously? Me in North Korea? Americans can visit, he said, and then I can be your guide. He seemed certain that he would be assigned to whatever tour group I ended up in. Admittedly, I knew folks who visited North Korea, but they all had dual citizenship. I only had my American passport. The whole thing seemed ludicrous, but J insisted that it wasn't. Just be cool, he said.

Beside, he added, folks will think you're just another one of the basketball players.

I smiled. Context was everything. When I moved to Venice from South Central, I remember how pissed I got whenever someone left a basketball or chicken bones on my front steps. I almost left a watermelon on the steps, just to psyche out whoever left the shit. I still wish I had. J's basketball comment, though, came from a very different place. Black basketball players *were* the in-thing in his country right now, all because Dear Leader, Jr. loved the sport and entertained the likes of Dennis Rodman. So maybe my black ass would fit in better than I thought.

We'll see, I said.

Of course, J hadn't been gone a full week before I started to pursue the possibility of a trip to Pyongyang. The idea of going there had always intrigued me, but now I had a purpose. I still felt very skeptical, though, that J would end up as one of my tour guides. First, I found out that one usually had two or three guides with them at all times. Second, how in the world would we ever hope to have alone time? Going to his place would be strictly forbidden. And I'm sure he would not be allowed in my hotel room. Still, none of this hard cold reality kept me from fantasizing about us making out on the top floor of the Ryugyong Hotel, the massive, 105-storied, pyramid-shaped carcass that has dominated the Pyongyang skyline, vacant, for over twenty year. It only recently received a skin of metal and glass over the grey concrete skeleton. It's said that the building sags and buckles from having been exposed to the elements for so long. What better place to have an illicit love affair?

So these fantasies, and just a desire to see J again, propelled me to go full-on with a plan to visit the Democratic People's Republic of Korea, the Workers' Paradise. Getting the time off was easy. I hadn't had a vacation for a while. Getting tickets to Beijing was a snap, too. That's where the journey began. The hardest part about getting to Pyongyang was finding the tour agency that arranged the trips. We had communicated via e-mail prior to my arrival in Beijing. Most of the details had been set. But finding the actual office took some doing. I stumbled on it only after several wrong turns. When I found it, I could see why it took a while to locate. The place looked like a rundown brothel from the outside.

Once I was there, though, the final arrangements fell quickly into place. I found myself whistling "Two Tickets to Paradise" while waiting for the bureaucratic wheels to turn.

In Pyongyang, I fell off the train groggy. It had been a long ride. I perked up quickly, though, because the first face I saw was J's. He clasped my hand with both of his. It felt like the warm hug he undoubtedly intended. Then he introduced me to the other tour guide, Song Jin-ju, and our driver Kim Tae-Hyun. I was the only member of this particular tour group, so it would be just the four of us. This happened sometimes, I was told. They were friendly with me at once and we all spoke on a given name basis. Tae-Hyun did not speak much English, but Jin, as she liked being called, was as fluent as J. And even she called him J, so I still did not find out his full name. Damn.

If the air smelled scented with a perfume I had never known, it was due to my looking into J's eyes as he looked into mine. A month apart had not dulled our mutual attraction. Our eyes gave each other deep tissue massages on the streets of his homeland.

Jin stepped between us. She looked like a schoolmarm, gently chiding her unruly students. "I'm sure you must be hungry," she said to me, "but first, it would be good for you to visit the statues of our Great Leaders, to pay homage."

I saw J nodding his head behind her.

"We usually request our visitors to lay flowers at the feet of our leaders," Jin explained. "Normally we do this the morning after arrival, but since it is still morning, we thought it best to do it now. That is, if you're not too tired."

"No, no, I'm fine," I said. Actually I had travel fatigue, but I didn't want to start the trip on the wrong foot. I thought it strange that this would be the very first thing we did, though. My impression of J was that he respected his country, but had a, shall we say, realistic view of his leaders. He never disparaged them when we were together in Malaysia, but he didn't seem convinced about their infallible. When we talked and held each other, and looked at the setting sun and starry skies, he told me about the fantastic tales associated with the Kims. How they rode on unicorns, how the earth trembled and the sky clapped with thunder at their every pronouncement. "Fantasies," he'd say. "All fantasies."

"It is important to maintain decorum," J said. "I hope you understand."

I nodded.

Tae-Hyun drove us as close as we could get, then we walked the rest of the way. Soon I found myself standing before two enormous bronze statues, one of each of the now-deceased Kims. Flowers adorned their feet.

Visions of fucking in the vacant pyramid hotel faded. Maybe my fatigue was getting the better of me, but I started to get annoyed. First, I had to buy my own flowers, €5. Then I had to listen and watch Jin explain the proper way of bowing and presenting the flowers. J watched as I learned all this ritual. His soft eyes had long vanished. He looked cold, officious. I began to think that coming was a bad idea.

I carried out my orders with nervous precision. I felt a marked man, like a bullet would take me out if I did something untoward. What if I coughed?

Or farted? Would that get me sent to the camps? J looked on, his stern expression providing me with no comfort. I was too out of my element. This isn't what I signed up for. I felt like his puppet.

As I robotically carried out my orders, J came up along side of me at the Kim Jong-Il statue. He did the bow, as solemnly as I had ever seen anyone bow, then he placed a small box filled with flower petals and oranges on the ground beneath the statue. After resting the box on the ground, he bowed again. Then he looked at me. His dimples returned along with a puckish grin. He winked an eye. The man I met in Malaysia returned. My fears abated. I bowed with him one final time. Jin and Tae-Hyun then came and left their tributes. Afterwards, we all removed ourselves from the feet of the Two Leaders.

We arrived at the hotel, the Yanggakdo on an island of the same name in the Taedong River. J accompanied me to the hotel room. He asked many times of the accommodations were OK. The room looked dated, like something from a 70s drama series, but it was clean and comfortable. I made a point of saying how much I liked it. That pleased J very much. "This is our best hotel," he said. I guess the large pyramid, the Ryugyong, was still closed. I didn't want to embarrass J by asking about it.

After we left the room, we went to another floor and met Jin and Tae-Hyun in a large banquet hall that could seat at least 80. I thought lunch would be a modest fair. Instead we feasted on a smorgasbord of food tastefully displayed. They had a variety of vegetable and tofu dishes to accommodate my vegetarian diet. And of course there was kimchi. J assured me that all lacked meat or chicken broth. We sat next to each other at a round table, with Jin and Tae-Hyun sitting opposite.

It all seemed too much. So much food for just four people in so large a room, I felt uncomfortable, knowing that just a few miles away were likely scores or event hundreds of people who wouldn't see an eighth this much food all day, or even during a week. But J seemed much more relaxed, even giddy. We all talked amiably about my travels. Tae-Hyun asked if I played basketball. I laughed and told him that I was terrible at it. I'm a tennis kinda guy, I said. He seemed disappointed. He wanted to learn some moves from me, I think.

J loved the comfortable banter. His officiousness vanished and his eyes caressed me again. At first it seemed awkward. I expected a guard or five to rush in and haul us away. But we had the large banquet room to ourselves. If Jin and Tae-Hyun noticed our eye flirtations, they were unfazed by them.

Four days went by quickly. We toured the city's major sites–Juche Tower, Arch of Reunification, the Grand People's Study House–and we also went out of town, to the DMZ and a palace where the Kims kept over 60 years worth of bling. Included was a limo given by Stalin to Kim Il-Sung.

The nights were the hardest, though. Each night, J accompanied me to my room. I'm not sure if this was normally allowed, but he did it without hesitation. "We have to make sure that you are comfortable," he said. On the second night, after a day of hard touring, we groped and kissed just inside the restroom. Hot passion controlled our hands and lips. We played music to drown us out, to thwart any listening devices. I call nights the hardest because, just as before, by the time I got used to his taste in my mouth, he had to leave. Staying in the room together for too long would have been dangerous for us both. But then I was alone, without his touch or taste. We never slept together a whole night back in Malaysia, but we did spend more quality time together there. Here, in his birth land, we had fleeting moments alone at best, and always tinged with the angst of discovery. Though in a way, that made it sort of exciting, like when I cruised Griffith Park back in the day.

J had a surprise on our last full day. Jin did not accompany us while Tae-Hyun drove J and me out of town and into the country. It seemed a strange, out of the way place to go. The air in the car inhibited questions, so I remained silent along with my travel companions. We stopped at a modest house on the edge of a wood. J and I got out. Then Tae-Hyun drove away.

"Come on," J said. "Hurry!"

We went into the house, which looked like it hadn't been lived in for quite some while. Sheets covered the furnishings and dust was everywhere. I tried a light switch, but there was no power. That didn't surprise me. There had been a few nights where the power in the hotel went out. We went into a smallish room with a single bed. J invited me to sit down. He then sat next to me and gave me the most passionate kiss I had ever known. Its length could be measured by years of pent up feelings and unexpressed emotions. I savored every moment of it, though when we stopped, and sat back a bit.

"Isn't this incredibly dangerous?"

"No," he said. "We won't be found here."

"I don't even know where 'here' is."

"My family once owned this land, long ago. There are rice patties about a kilometer away. I may be working there later, after you have gone home. So I knew of this place, and have come here often. You are the first I have brought here."

His smiling dimples set my heart afire, though I still had reservations.

"But if we're caught. . ."

"There are no bugs here, like in your room. And no one comes here. Think of this as our Griffith Park."

We made love, long hot passionate, sweaty, sticky, messy love. It was the type of love that teens have their first time. It was the sort of love that one read about in romance novels. I don't think it was J's first time with a man–lord knows it wasn't mine. Yet that's what it felt like for the both of us. Then he explained it all to me. When we made our tributes to the Dear Leaders, it was in the manner of newlyweds after their wedding. Then we followed that with a wedding banquet. He said that Jin helped to arrange it all, just as she provided cover for us while we carried on in this abandoned house. "She's like a sister to me."

After a couple of hours, Tae-Hyun returned to fetch us. We both straightened up our clothes as best we could, neatened our disheveled hair. Our driver said nothing as we entered the car, though I thought I caught a wry grin on his face. Did he know? We remained silent during the drive back into town. Somehow, no one seemed to notice or care that a black dude rode in a car so far off the beaten path I didn't ask what sort of cover Jin provided for us. I figured the less I knew the better.

During our goodbyes, I asked J if he would ever travel abroad again. He said possibly. He still had his mother to consider. I think he wanted me to meet his mother, but that would have been near impossible to arrange. Harder, even, than our tryst in his family's ancestral house, which I dubbed Griffith House.

It's been nearly a year since that encounter. I have no way of contacting J or finding out indirectly what he's doing. Even if I knew his full name, I wouldn't google it, fearing that someone might track my searches back to him and get him into trouble. My mind still fills with fantasies about him, his flesh, his sweet nature. I worry about his fate. Sometimes I wonder if he's a distant relative of the Kim family, which would explain the freedoms he seemed to enjoy. But on the other hand, Dear Leader, Jr. just bumped off his uncle for "dreaming different dreams." I didn't like reading about the gory details, speculation that he fed his uncle to ravenous dogs. Such things were known to happen to gay folks in Nazi Germany.

It would have been much easier for us to have had sex while in Malaysia. No one would have been the wiser. There were no bugs in my room there, no guards checking in on us. But eventually, I figured out why he waited until I came to Pyongyang. I was his fantasy, his unicorn, his clap of thunder in a portentous sky. He wanted our love to be an act of civil disobedience, carried out almost literally under the noses of the giant bronze statues of the Kims.

I hope he didn't have to pay the price for it. I hope to one day see my Dear Beloved Comrade again.

TWO VISITORS

VINCENT TRAUGHBER MEIS

His mother sat by his bed and said little. All her words of mothering—to be a good man, to make her proud, to bring honor to the family, to give her grandchildren—had been exhausted on his two older brothers who had given her six grandchildren and at least that many disappointments. The journalist son was in prison, an "enemy of the people," and the oldest son was married to a woman with modern ideas. She was exhausted all the time now and offered her third son, Ali, simply her motherly love and the promise to visit as often as she could.

That first time she came to him in the darkest hours of night when the veil on reality was the thinnest, the hours of evil spirits, he was afraid. But she didn't convert into a djinn before his eyes or inhabit his body, forcing him to do horrible things. She gave him comfort, her presence alone giving him a respite from his loneliness.

She cupped a hand under his chin like she used to do when he was a little boy. "Have you eaten well today?" she asked and then as if suddenly realizing he wasn't a little boy anymore, took back her hand to rearrange her scarf, tucking the sides in to get the slippery material off her face.

Ali nodded. She didn't need to know the truth or how long it had been since he had eaten well. He had waited all afternoon on the bridge, scanning the horizon for the supply boat, which now only came when there were donations since the shipping company's credit had long run out and he had no funds to pay himself. When the word got out that he was in need, the people of the town had taken pity and collected provisions for him in the Arabic tradition of taking care of a guest. At first, he had more than he needed. But as days became weeks became months became years, he was sometimes forgotten. He imagined it was the same all over the world that after a time guests begin to smell like old fish as the saying goes. He had recently marked the two-year anniversary on his floating prison, anchored offshore with a view of normal life in the seaside town and the prayer call easily heard from the minarets. Two years since he had seen his family. Two years since his career as a first mate on the MV Rakan had come to a halt, his sailing to ports from Hong Kong to Casablanca suspended.

His constant hunger made him dream of food, his mother's cooking, her muhammara and kibbeh making his mouth go watery and he reached for a pita to scoop up the shiny red pepper paste, drool dripping from the corners of his mouth.

The blast of a passing ship erased the food and made him sit up with the pangs of hunger more powerful than ever. The wake of the other ship gently rocked him as he wiped the saliva from his chin and threw off the blanket. She sat at a distance now across the room in the wobbly desk chair, the whites of her dark eyes catching a petal of moonlight, her hands lost in the sleeves of the opposite arms. She looked sad or tired or unwell.

He swung his legs over the side of the bed and his feet searched the floor for his red Moroccan babouche slippers intricately carved with a floral design. His rough feet scratched against the soft grain of the leather, and he kicked them out of sight under the bed. He didn't want to chance that his mother would ask where they came from, if they were a gift and from whom. As she could see through his lies, he must avoid the subject, the unbearable notion that she might discover the person lurking deep inside that he had never shown the world. The slippers, now laced with the sweat and oil of his feet, had mysteriously appeared in his closet one day after the stop in the port of Ceuta, a mystery easily solved. He had admired the slippers when he and a mate from the ship walked through the old medina. "Treat yourself to something nice," said the companion.

"I could not," said Ali. It was not in his nature to wear anything showy except for his merchant marine uniform in which he felt most comfortable. His casual clothes were colorless and baggy.

Why was his mother now sitting so far away across the room, her image and the comfort of her presence diminished? So many things didn't make sense these days. He couldn't think clearly. In these hours of not-yet-morning, his memory was also soft, malleable like the dough his mother prepared and kneaded for pita bread. "How is my daughter?" he asked. "How is little Esme?"

She turned her head and looked out the small round window. In the darkness he could only make out her silhouette, and with her eyes now turned away, he didn't know what they were saying, the eyes that at times had reduced him to dust and at others cast him in a beam of love, her youngest son, the eye of her eye.

"And what of little Esme?" he asked again.

She remained silent.

He fingered the scratchy blanket, the roughness sending a memory ripping through him of Esme complaining about the scratchiness of her blanket. The next day he had gone to the market and bought her the softest one he could find. He had told his wife, Yasmin, not to go to Aleppo that day, not to take Esme to visit her grandparents who were crazy to see her.

His mother slowly rose to her feet to take her leave. "*Ma' assalama*, eye of my eye," she said in a voice as delicate as the threads of fine silk of her scarf. Her dark clothes fluttered into the shadows and then she was no more. He banged his fists against his forehead and from the edge of the bed fell forward onto his boney knees. He touched his forehead to the floor as if he was praying, but it wasn't time yet. He swiveled around and reached under the bed, his fingers brushing over rat droppings before landing on the slippers, which he retrieved and slipped onto his feet, encasing them in a bit of nostalgia he had tried but could not give up. Why should he not wear the red slippers? No one would see him. He was alone in the world's largest single-occupancy prison, a cargo ship a hundred meters long with a breadth of eighteen meters. As the first mate, he knew everything about the ship, its immense physicality, its secret passages, its instruments, but now in his isolation was learning the horrors of it, its possession by spirits that taunted him.

He sat again on the edge of the bed and switched on his phone. Two notifications. The first informed him that it was ten minutes until *fajr salah*, sunrise prayer time; the second that his battery was at five percent. No messages from the outside world. He quickly shut it off and shuffled to the pail of water that sat in the sink—the ship's plumbing had long since stopped functioning without power—to begin his ablutions as the call from the minarets on land would soon begin. As he splashed water on his hands and arms, the five percent of his battery flashed as an afterimage in the half-darkness, shaking him with its warning. The phone was his connection to the outside world. The phone told him when to pray. The phone held photos—he and Eric walking in the medina of Ceuta and posing with arms around each other at landmarks in Marseille—his memories, his sins.

The last time he had spoken to his mother by phone he lamented that he could never talk long due to his fading battery. She laughed. "When I was young, your father wrote me letters. So much better." As soon as the call ended, he swept through the living quarters, sifting through the detritus of the departed crew and came up with pens chewed at the end, wrinkled paper, and yellowing envelopes. He started a letter to his mother in the formal Arabic he had been taught in school, but was unhappy with it, crumpling up draft after draft. How to be both respectful and intimate was a challenge. He wanted to communicate how important she was in his life without sounding soft, the baby of the family, the eye of her eye as she always told him. His brothers often teased him about being soft.

As he sat at his desk, letting the pen scratch sluggishly across the paper, he marveled in the calligraphy of his language, stunning on the page, but also the beauty of being able to say things that he couldn't in a phone call or text. Still, after many days of writing, he was unsure as he sealed the envelope if she would be pleased, if he had said everything he wanted to say, if he had found the right tone. "So many steps to writing a letter," he mumbled to himself. In his predicament, the production of the letter was one thing; the mailing of it was quite another.

He would have to swim to land with the letter in a sealed plastic pouch, held inside his shirt and tucked in the waistband of his shorts, early in the morning when the shipyard guard he knew was on duty, the one whose palm he greased with a few dollars when he had it so that he would look the other way when Ali went through the gate into the town.

On the day of mailing his mother's letter, he checked the rope and wooden ladder to make sure it was secured to the deck and then threw it over the side. It hit the water with a loud splash, but no one was on the beach who might notice. He began the long descent, not looking down but instead at the hull of the ship, which was in bad shape, rusted and corroded, paint faded and chipping. Colors swirled in front of his eyes, splotches of light blue and dark blue and orange and red and brown and yellow that made him think of a modern painting he had seen with Eric. When they had arrived in the port of Marseille, the captain announced they had a few hours of shore leave. Most of the crew headed for shopping malls, bars, and brothels, but Eric convinced Ali to go to a museum. Ali had never been to a western museum and feared what he might encounter. In the Musée des Beaux-Arts, they stood in front of a painting of two men standing next to a wall with the water of the bay in the background. It was the multi-colored depiction of the water that Ali thought of as he climbed down the ladder staring at the hull.

"The man in the red turban looks like you, Ali," said Eric. The man had dark hair and an angular face. He wore a long coat with brass buttons that could have been a military or seaman's coat.

"The European one looks nothing like you," said Ali. It was an older man with a thick white beard and wore a heavy leather coat and a large-billed flat cap.

"That is true. Maybe when I'm much older, but I don't think I will ever have such a beard." Eric ran his hand over his smooth face and chuckled.

"Let's move on. I don't like the way this man is looking at me." The devil's eyes of the older man of the painting followed him even when he changed his position. The next painting portrayed a nearly naked boy playing a lyre. This one did look like Eric with pale hairless limbs that stabbed Ali's heart with a memory from that morning. He hurried past it.

"Wait. Would you look at that! This is me. A musician. It's Orpheus. Sweet as." Eric wrote songs in his free time on the ship and hoped to be a singer one day.

"I don't like this. It is frightening." The boy in the painting was in a hellish place with other half-naked people and beasts. "In Islamic art, we don't much represent the human form, especially with no clothes."

"It is said that Orpheus could charm all living things and even the rocks with his music. He went into the underworld in hopes of using his music skills to retrieve his wife who died." Ali tensed up, and Eric reached out to touch his arm. "I'm sorry. I wasn't thinking."

Ali shook off Eric's hand. "It is nothing. Can we go, please?"

On the way out of the museum, they passed through a room where a ray of light shot through a skylight and landed on a statue of a bare-breasted woman in the center. Ali sped by the statue and hurried toward the exit.

Eric followed after him, trying to suppress a giggle. "What's the matter, mate?"

"I do not understand this what you call art."

Ali reached the bottom of the ladder and jumped in the water. It wasn't deep. He swam less than a hundred yards to a point where he could stand up. He made it to the beach where he had to step over debris and trash stirred up by the storm. Like a monster emerging from the sea, seaweed and plastic bags clinging to soaking clothes and sneakers, he made his way to the pier that led to the shipyard. He didn't need to worry about the guard as he was snoring loudly in the booth.

With the post office not opening for a couple of hours, he went to the Internet café where he could charge his phone and check his email without running down the battery. He had a few piastres left to pay for the service and a few more to pay for the stamp.

From the café, he made his way in the shadows down alleys until he reached the drab little cinderblock post office, which was still closed. He sat on the ground to wait. Twenty minutes later the postal clerk limped down the road and eyed Ali suspiciously.

"*As-salamu alaykum,*" Ali said to the man.

"*Wa alaykumu s-salam,*" the clerk mumbled. He neither acted surprised to see Ali nor offered an excuse for being late. Ali started to follow him into the building, but he held up his hand and motioned for him to wait outside. Ali was anxious to get back to the ship before the streets came to life, before the carts of vegetables rolled to the markets and fish sellers barked their prices, before the police awakened from their morning naps and began their strolls through the streets. He had already been stopped on previous ventures into the town and threatened arrest for abandoning the ship. "Arrest me," Ali had told them. "The jail can't be worse than my prison on the ship." He had been tricked into signing a document of responsibility for the ship until the fines were paid, two years since the Egyptian Port authorities came aboard with documents concerning the detention of the ship. Ali had called the captain who had conveniently gone ashore, and the captain told him to sign the documents. By signing, Ali unwittingly made himself the sole legal guardian of the ship until the issues were resolved. The authorities made him relinquish his passport, making it impossible for him to leave the country. Every time Ali thought of the captain, he would spit to ward off the evil like he always did when he encountered a black cat. He was still furious with the man who had never returned to his ship and had never contacted Ali to offer an explanation.

Of course, the police didn't want the responsibility of arresting him or caring for him in the jail. Normally if they caught sight of him on the streets, they pretended as if they did not.

The temperature rose several degrees in the time before the postal clerk finally waved him into the office and surprised him by putting a small box on the counter in front of him. He gawked at the label, realizing that it was, in fact, for him. The return address said Los Angeles, California, and considering how many times his family had send things, which never arrived, he was amazed that the package had traveled so far. It was the solar cell phone charger his uncle in the United States had promised him. "*Al hamdulillah,*" he said.

Not wanting to risk the swim back with his precious cargo despite having the plastic pouch, he hurried to the docks where the fishing boats came in. He had managed to barter with some of the fishermen, exchanging things from the ship for fish; he had a cache of items—cooking utensils, rope, and little treasures crew members had bought on shopping trips but had been left behind in their haste to leave the ship. A few of the items crew members had asked him to put in the company safe were still there. One was a necklace he had planned on giving his mother when he went home. It wasn't a necklace of true value, only fake diamonds from one of the stalls in the Ceuta market.

Ali found a fisherman he knew who had told him about his love for a local girl and liked to give her gifts to win her heart. The last time Ali had traded a large cooking pot from the galley for some of the man's fish. This time he offered him the necklace for shuttling him back to the ship. The fisherman was weary after a night of fishing, but Ali convinced him it would be worth his while. When they got to the ship and Ali showed him the necklace, the fisherman's eyes sparkled, and he threw a few fish into the bargain.

Ali connected his phone and placed it in a sunny spot on deck. He sat reading nearby in the shade but kept glancing at it to make sure it was charging. It was not at a hundred percent by nightfall, but it was the best charge he had had in a long time. He celebrated by cooking the fish on his makeshift grill, burning wood from the ship's furniture he smashed into pieces. He also prepared a cup of tea from a bag he had been hoarding. He was delirious with happiness and decided to call his mother. The phone rang many times, but there was no answer.

In the darkest hour, Ali awoke to find that Allah in his eternal grace and wisdom had allowed him a second visitor. Or was it a test? Temptation lay beside him, the heat of another body, the smell of the sandalwood soap Eric bought in Marseille. His heart raced while his mind was thrown into confusion.

"How are you, *habibi?*" said Eric. Ali regretted teaching him the word of endearment because of the power it had over him.

"I am fine. But I cannot lie with you like this. It is wrong."

Eric touched Ali's forehead, ran his finger along the bridge of his nose, and rested it on Ali's lips. "We've been through this. What possible harm can this cause? There is so much cruelty and pain in the world. Are we not allowed a little pleasure?"

Eric moved his hand down to Ali's heart and felt the pounding. On the outside Ali was frozen, but inside he burned with the memory of Eric's lips that drugged him with a secret potion, his golden curls that wrapped around his fingers and wouldn't let go, his lithe body that lay under him and begged to be filled.

"You deserve this, Ali. You have suffered so much." Eric slipped his hand, chafed from his kitchen work, under Ali's shirt and ran it back and forth over his chest as if trying to smooth over his doubts. The slight roughness of Eric's fingers made his skin tingle with pleasures like finding the exact spot on your back that itches and scratching it with sweet relief. Eric brushed his right nipple, causing Ali to shudder and shake his head, whispering, "No, no." All his prayers in making these feelings go away had been useless.

Eric's hand was now in his underwear, massaging him to life, breaking down the last stones of the wall, turning them to dust. Ali's need for touch was consuming him with a power all its own, making his hands reach for the back of Eric's head and bring his lips to his, hungry for the potion that sent the blood rushing through his veins. In a moment, Eric had removed his shorts and thrust his head between Ali's legs. Ali's fingers were entwined with Eric's soft curls, which he remembered shining in the light that first day he saw him, and as Eric's head moved up and down, he held on and gasped for breath, his heart thumping against his ribcage. This vile act, Eric taking him into his mouth, was unlike anything he had experienced in his life; no one else had ever done this to him. Was it so pleasurable because it was so vile, leading him into a life of sin, taking him to a place from which he would never be able to return? But after Eric was gone from the ship, he had returned to the righteous path, had praised Allah five times a day and brought his desires back under control, back to the control he had exhibited all his life, controlling his feelings, controlling his actions, controlling his thoughts.

The door closed and he sat on the side of the bed, elbows on his knees, his weighty head resting in his palms, waiting for Ali Mostafa, Chief Mate, to return to his body. Nothing remained of his pale friend but the bleachy odor of sex and sweat of men. He stood up, hurried to the pail in his bathroom, and splashed water on his face, his neck. He grabbed a washcloth and wiped his limp dick, causing it to shrivel further with the cold water, his balls to contract, sending a shiver through him. He dabbed frantically at the dried semen crusted on his inner thigh. Why was he so weak?

Several months before the ship was detained, the company informed Ali they would be taking on a new messman at the port in Perth. It was Ali's job to officially welcome the Australian. Despite having glanced over Eric's files and profile picture, he was shocked when the pale young man with golden hair and blue eyes walked into the chief mate's office. The previous messman had been Filipino, and the cook had privately expressed his surprise that the new hire was a break in the tradition of having someone from the Philippines fill the position. Ali wondered why an educated young man like Eric, a citizen of a first world country would want a job on a third-rate shipping company vessel with an Egyptian captain, a Syrian chief mate, a Filipino cook and the rest of the crew made up of Indians, Pakistanis, Chinese, two Iraqis, a Sri Lankan, and an Ethiopian. He shared nothing with the rest of the crew in terms of culture, and, Ali guessed, interests. And physically, he was like a delicate yellow rose in a garden of plants with dark shiny leaves.

At the first sight of Eric, Ali felt an immediate dip in his stomach like a ship riding the downside of a wave of a big storm, that sense of losing control. He treated Eric coolly and ignored the strange feeling in his gut.

Eric kept to himself and did his work well. The cook was happy he could delegate many of the kitchen chores to him with complete confidence. There were no complaints about his cleaning duties of the messroom or officers' quarters. Ali overheard the crew make a few disparaging remarks about Eric's aloofness, his longish hair, which he wore pulled back and under a hat, and his fluid mannerisms, but as long as there were no overt conflicts, he didn't intercede.

One evening in port several weeks after Eric's arrival, Ali smoked a cigarette on deck in the still night air and noticed down the way the glow at the end of another cigarette turning a bright orange with someone's intake of smoke. "Hello, mate," said a voice, and then the glow moved toward him.

Ali felt a slight uptake in his heartbeat. "Is that you, Eric?"

"Good evening, sir. Lovely night, isn't it?"

"Yes. I think we would see a lot of stars if there weren't so many lights in the port. You didn't want to go ashore with the others?"

Eric snorted. "Yeah. No. Not my thing." The main reasons for going ashore were whoring or shopping. They spoke quietly and dragged on their cigarettes. When their cigarettes were nearly finished, Ali was relieved it would be time to put them out and move on. He thought of some business he needed to attend to.

Eric threw the butt of his cigarette over the rail into the bay. "Life at sea must be difficult for a married man."

Ali was shaken by the personal turn. "How do you...?"

"I saw your ring."

"You know my country is in a terrible war?"

"I don't know much about it."

"Many people have died."

"Terrible, yes. I'm sorry."

Ali had never opened up to anyone on the ship and tried to stop himself from doing it now. Something about Eric being from a different world and standing close and the strange physical reaction Ali had to his presence and the quiet night and his exhaustion from holding it inside made him start talking. Words flowed, a stream of sadness from his mouth that could not be stopped until the story had been told.

"My wife and daughter went to visit the grandparents in Aleppo. They were supposed to return before nightfall, but the roads were blocked. They stayed with my sister-in-law that night, and the bombs fell. People tell me they felt no pain."

Eric hesitated as if conjuring an appropriate response to such a devastating revelation. "Sorry for your loss, mate. I can't imagine."

"My oldest brother allowed me no time to grieve. He dragged me out of bed, drove me to the marine school in Jordan, and paid for my tuition. If I had stayed in the country, I might have done something stupid against the government that ordered the attacks. Our middle brother was in prison and the oldest had to make sure I didn't end up there too. That's how I started in the merchant marines."

"Good thing you left. You could have been killed and we wouldn't be here having this convo. I lost an uncle I was very close to, but I realize it's not the same."

As they talked quietly, the wisps of smoke from their cigarettes traveled up in the still air and wrapped around each other like two ghosts embracing. The ship was so quiet they could hear the waves sloshing against the side and they leaned over the railing, their hands nearly touching.

Ali sat on deck under a shade awning he had rigged up though the heat wasn't bad with the gentle breeze that blew over him, reminding him of home and the cool air that would sweep down from the coastal mountains. Next to him but outside the shade sat the solar charger soaking up the sun. He shooed away the pesky flies that constantly landed on him, his face, his nose, in the corner of his eye. During certain seasons of the year, the flies also bit him, tiny pricks on his skin. At night, it was the mosquitoes forcing him inside when he wanted to watch the moon come up.

It was almost time for the Asr *salah* and he would soon hear the speakers crackle, and then the call would begin from the minarets rising above the dusty town on the port side of the ship. His rug was laid out ready and the little pail of water was nearby for his ablutions. He preferred to use fresh water for *wudu* than sea water, which wasn't clean in the port, but he had to use the water sparingly, sprinkling a few drops on his hands, arms, face, head, and feet. Eric probably wouldn't understand his need to adhere to the five prayer times. They had once talked about the importance of prayer, but Eric, an infidel, clearly didn't understand. They're best moments had been when they were quiet, lying on the bed, staring at the ceiling, holding hands. He was appalled that thoughts of Eric would come into his head as he prepared for prayer and he tried to rid his mind of them.

The biting flies had put him in a foul mood. These days small things sent him tumbling into his dark space of wondering if Eric provoked the captain like in the story the captain had told in a drunken state. The official report stated that Eric had been despondent and jumped from the ship into the water and drowned. But the chief engineer told Ali a very different story. The captain and the engineer had gotten drunk one night, and the captain claimed Eric had approached him for sex, and when the captain refused, they struggled. Eric had slipped and fallen over the side.

Ali knew the captain to be an untrustworthy man and believed neither the official version nor the drunken version of Eric's drowning. Eric had told him the captain flirted with him on several occasions, but Eric adamantly expressed he had no interest. Once, as he cleaned the captain's quarters, the captain surprised him and tried to force himself on him. Eric wanted to file an official complaint, but Ali convinced him not to. There were no witnesses, and it would be the captain's word against a new employee who everyone assumed was a homosexual. But in the twisted tangle of nerves inside Ali, his doubts made him not want to pursue the matter. The emotions Eric stirred up in him could be stirred up in others as well; perhaps the captain had come under the same spell.

But in moments of great loneliness, Ali would go to his phone and pull up pictures of them together, experiencing a deep sadness for the loss of his friend. Remembering the joyful moments they shared brought him to tears. One day, standing at the open window on the bridge, looking out on the view that changed little from season to season, the shoreline and the small town in tones of brown, gray, and beige, the gulf water a pale green, he prayed to Allah to give him a sign that his feelings were not evil. The ship creaked and swayed in tiny ways he detected as if it were his outer skin, part of him. He felt its movements in his bones. The ship was sick, rusting, dam-aged. Like his soul. But still, he had hope for a sign.

In the afternoon, he heard the motor of a small boat. It was a representa-tive from a relief organization, bringing him food, water, batteries for his lamp, and other supplies. The man shouted up to him, "Praise Allah," and Ali responded with "God is great."

Was this the sign he hoped for? Maybe God was rewarding him for be-ing a good man and he was allowed his feelings because they didn't hurt anyone. He was a peaceful man. He was a devout man. He had been a good husband and father. The cruel punishment, the death of his wife and daugh-ter, had come before he touched Eric, before he imagined touching a man. Even as a boy, he didn't participate in the games of discovery other boys did. He was so ignorant about sex he went to his brother the night before his wedding, asking him what he had to do.

His mother used to tell the story of how much she wanted a girl when she realized she was pregnant for the third time. His two older brothers were difficult babies and later frequently got in trouble, exhausting the parents. His mother even went to a woman who made potions to make sure pregnant women got the sex they wanted. From his first moment of life, he felt that he had failed in some way, and though he couldn't see his parents' expressions, he sensed in his tiny baby soul something was wrong. In later years, his mother would tell the story of how his father held him saying he loved him even if he wasn't a girl. He had been put on notice; he knew he had to be extra good and never fail his parents. But as good as he was, life gave him punishment after punishment. And still he tried harder. When this current trial was over, he would go back out to sea and become a captain. His father was no longer able to work, and he bore some of the responsibility to care for his ailing father and the younger sister his parents were finally blessed with. He could not fail them. He could not shame them. He would no longer communicate with Eric who had fallen under the enchantment of Iblis, leader of the devils. The gift from heaven of the food and supplies was a tease, not really a sign.

But later his weakness took hold of him and he went to his phone again, each photo stabbing his heart, each photo producing another tear.

The call of the muezzin shook him from his sorry state, coming from the various mosques in the area, not all at once but in rolling waves of sound one over the other. The first one began with "*Allahu Akhbar.*" A few seconds later, the call rang out from a minaret farther to the north. And then another and another. He dipped his hands into the small pail and wiped them over his face. He dipped again and ran his hands over his arms up to and including his elbows. With his still wet hands he touched the top of his head. One more dip and he dribbled water over his feet rubbing them up to his ankles. He stood upright in the middle of his rug facing Mecca and initiated the *takbir* with "Allah is the greatest." He bowed at the waist and put his hands on his knees. His feet were shoulder-width apart and he stared at the space between his feet, waiting God's command. "Glory be to Allah, the most magnificent," he whispered. Then he descended to his knees and in full prostration, he touched his forehead and nose to the ground with his hands on either side of his ears. "Glory be to Allah the almighty." He returned to a sitting position with his legs tucked under him. In this position, he begged for forgiveness of his sins, especially his one big sin, his lustful thoughts about Eric. He bent down again in full prostration, but was distracted by the pattern in the carpet, two blue flowers side by side, the trusting eyes of Eric staring up at him like that first time he sat on Eric's prone body and leaned down to kiss him, fireworks going off in his head, his heart about to explode.

Ali felt the disgust of a hundred beasts running through his body, and he jumped up and slapped himself across the face. He swirled around as if he expected to see the devil at his shoulder. He went back to the water pail, and though he regretted using the precious water, he would have to restart his *wudu*. He was unclean. He had ruined his *salah* with his lurid thoughts. He reached for the solar charger attached to the phone and threw it overboard. It was a cursed object.

After the ship was detained, the other crew members had left, one by one, some of them staying for months in hopes the legal issues would be resolved and they would get paid. None of them had received their salary since the port authorities had found faults with the ship. A merchant marine representative said the owner of the ship had stopped communicating and a resolution looked unlikely. The chief engineer from India was the last to go.

Weeks after the engineer left, Ali started having visitors. On a warm September evening, Ali felt a presence outside his quarters. He opened the door, surprised to see his mother. "*Ummi*, come in." Her long dress hung on her like her shoulders were too weak to hold it up. Her eyes receded into her skull. "Are you not well?"

She made a shooing gesture and followed him into the room. "Your brother has been released. His body is still bruised and his face scarred, but he is alive. We try to find a way he can leave the country."

"Yes, it is for the best."

She looked around the room. "Has someone else been here?"

"No, of course not. Why?" he said harshly.

She looked taken aback by his abrupt answer. "There is a new smell. Sandalwood. And those red slippers."

Panic seized Ali's throat as he struggled for an explanation. "I find things in the quarters of the departed crew, things they left behind. A bar of soap. Slippers. If I am lucky, I find toothpaste."

She shook her head but appeared too weary to continue her interrogation. "Your other brother writes many letters to agencies of the government to help your case, but nothing."

Ali was reminded of the letter he wrote to her. "Did you get my letter?"

"You wrote me a letter, eye of my eye?"

"Yes, weeks ago."

"Nothing works in our country. We are lucky if we get mail once a week. Your brother sometimes gets letters that have been opened by the censors."

"How is my little sister?"

"In love with a soldier. Your brother forbids it. But let us not talk of such things. You must make peace with God and you will find a way home." She stared at the red slippers.

"I pray five times every day. There is no temptation here. Only loneliness."

There was a noise in the hallway. "Are you expecting someone?" she said.

He was grateful Eric and his mother had never crossed paths in their visits. If Eric was in the hall, he would know, hearing the voice of his mother, not to enter. "I told you. No one comes here. It is only the rats." His words came out too strong, a hint of disrespect to his mother.

She took a step back with a look of pain on her face.

"I'm sorry, mother. I'm weary of this life." He bowed his head and covered his eyes with his hand. When he looked up, she was gone. He grabbed his flashlight from the nightstand and rushed into the hall. A figure turned the corner, not dressed in dark colors like his mother, but a small person in a yellow dress. She turned a corner, and Ali hurried after her, calling out, "Esme? Esme?" The door was open to Eric's old room, and he went in. There was no one in the room, but the door slammed suddenly. He struggled to open it again. When he got back into the hallway, another figure moved away from him. "Yasmin?" The flashlight dimmed and then lost power, leaving him in oppressive darkness. He heard raspy breathing, and a hand landed on his shoulder, causing him to spin around. "Mother?" He could see nothing. He reached out and touched a wall, cold and damp. With his hands desperately running along the walls, he staggered back to his room, entered, and slammed the door.

He collapsed on his foul-smelling bed and hugged himself, remembering that first morning, not yet light, when Eric came to his cabin. As the messman on his way to begin preparations for breakfast, no one would be suspicious of his movements about the ship. There was a light tap on his metal door, breaking into his dream only to give him a new one, a real one. Nothing had been arranged, but he knew who it was. After their cigarette conversation, there had been furtive looks at meetings and when they passed each other in the hallways. There was something in those blue eyes, a mystery, a door to another place that frightened him.

Though Eric's touch at the door was soft, to Ali it sounded like the clanging of the ship's alarm, and he jumped out of bed. The door groaned as he opened it, and he pulled Eric in. He was surprised and not surprised. Eric had the shy, affable demeanor of someone who rarely left the shadows, knowing what dangers lurked if he showed himself in the light. And yet that flash of profound longing Ali had seen that night of their cigarettes as the port lights reflected in his eyes must have propelled him to leave his zone of comfort. Ali, for his part, played reluctance, telling himself that pulling Eric into the room with such force was to avoid a scandal in the unlikely case someone happened by at that hour.

"What are you doing here?" Ali whispered.

Eric chuckled. "Are we going to play that game?" A ray of moonlight beamed in the porthole and made Eric's pale face glisten with sweat. Ali cowered under his gaze and turned his head toward a bulletin board on the wall with schedules, notices, reminders, and a picture of his wife and daughter.

The wound of losing his family was still raw, and he longed for the touch of another person, someone who might make him feel human again. In the dark where no one would see, it didn't matter who it was, or so it seemed at the time. Still, he couldn't look at him.

Eric touched his face and tried to move his head to face him. "You can tell me to go."

Ali stood like a statue, rocking delicately with the movement of the ship as if he might topple over. Eric took his hand. "Ali?"

Eric's hand was warm and electric, sending sparks up Ali's arm. He imagined being in an electric chair like he had seen in a movie, feeling the first surges of the destruction that was to come. He gasped as if it was his last breath and fell back on the bed, drawing Eric on top of him. Eric's mouth smelled of mint and his hair of herbs, taking him to a mountain meadow before the war, escaping the summer heat with his family, picnic on the grass, his daughter picking flowers, the sky abundant with the threat of rain. He allowed Eric to kiss him, but he couldn't let go yet. Though Eric didn't weigh much, the pressure pushing down on him felt like the incubus of a dream.

"I can't...I can't breathe."

Eric rolled over and lay on his back. "I'll go." He started to get up.

Ali grabbed his arm. "I am not...I've never..."

Eric sat on the edge of the bed, his forearm still in Ali's desperate grip. "What? No playing around with other boys. You would be the first Arab I've heard of that didn't."

"This is different. I mean since my..."

"How is this different?"

"We aren't boys. I still feel married."

In the last two weeks, the food supply had dwindled almost to nothing. He ate stale saltines with the last can of sardines he had hoarded. He regretted throwing his phone overboard, but there was nothing he could do about it. The spirits on the ship had gotten stronger, and he no longer left his quarters as he feared the noises and voices in the hallways of ship. He was too weak to pray, the one thing that had kept him sane for so long. And then, what he feared most happened. His two visitors crossed paths. Eric was on one side of the bed and his mother on the other. He was stretched out with his hands crossed over his chest in a dead man's pose.

"Why do you not answer your phone?" said Eric. "I've called you many times."

He turned his head toward Eric with a blank stare as if he didn't know him.

His mother pulled her scarf over her nose and mouth. The smell of his unwashed body permeated the room. When she spoke, the silk fluttered with the breath of her speaking. "When was the last time you ate, eye of my eye?"

He raised his hand a few inches to make a sign but dropped it back to his chest as he had no strength. Nor could he speak. He looked down at his feet and shame overtook him when he saw he wore his red slippers. His mother's eyes followed his, landing on his feet.

Ali felt the vessel move, lurching to one side as it did in a storm. "The ship is moving," he mumbled.

Eric leaned forward. "What did you say, habibi?"

His mother put her hand to her face as if she had just been slapped. Ali felt her eyes crushing him. "Your friend?"

"The ship is floating out to sea," Ali managed in a whisper, irritating his parched throat.

His mother now put the back of her hand to Ali's forehead, checking for fever. She looked at Eric and nodded.

Ali took her hand gently in his and smiled, sure that he had a new visitor, his wife who had once comforted him when he had a high temperature. It seemed she hadn't gone to Aleppo after all. "Where is Esme?" he whispered.

Again, his mother and Eric shared a glance of concern as if their desire for his well-being erased their differences.

Ali closed his eyes, and when he opened them, the door burst open and two men entered with a look of horror on their faces at the smell, the state of Ali's frail body, his unshaven face and vacant eyes.

"We have come for you, Ali," said one of them, a port policemen who knew him, who in the early months of his confinement had visited him frequently. But as time went on, he had been forgotten. "The replacement has been approved. You're going home."

The other man searched the room and opened drawers for a change of clothes, at least something marginally cleaner than what he was wearing.

"Home?" said Ali as if it was a new word for him. He looked to either side of his bed. His visitors had vanished. Perhaps these men were just a dream.

The policeman pointed to the other man. "This is Hadi, a union representative who will take your place, and the Egyptian authorities have agreed. Can you sit up?"

After doing a smell test on several articles of clothing scattered around the room, Hadi opened up his bag and pulled out one of his own T-shirts and a pair of sweatpants.

They got Ali sitting up on the side of the bed, but, when they tried to remove his shirt, he resisted though he was too fragile to put up much of a fight. They changed his clothes and put a bottle of water to his lips, telling him to drink slowly.

With one man on each side of him, they walked him down the hall out of the living quarters and onto the deck where the rosy morning sky produced enough light to make Ali shield his eyes with his hand while he groaned with the prickly brightness overwhelming his retinas. The call to *fajr* prayer rang out from the minarets, and Ali gestured toward the area with the awning he had rigged up and the prayer rug bunched in a corner, swept there by the wind. "I must pray," he said. It had been a pair of weeks since he had last done *salah*.

The two men shared a glance of uncertainty. He was in no condition to complete the ritual. "Traveling is a legitimate reason to skip prayers," said Hadi. "You can do the next one at midday."

The two men propped Ali up on an equipment box by the railing while they looked over the edge at the ladder down to the waiting coast guard boat. Ali was too weak to descend the rope ladder on his own. "Ali, we will strap you to my back, but you must hold on with your arms to go down the ladder," said Hadi.

Ali's head hung down and his eyes were half open. The words of the muezzin continued from the minaret, flowing out over the water. His head began to bob to the words.

The policeman grabbed Ali firmly by the shoulder. "Do you understand?"

Ali opened his eyes a little wider. "*Ana aasef.*" I'm sorry.

"Don't worry. You are going home."

Hadi climbed down the ladder and got rope from the boat and climbed back up. They put Ali on Hadi's back and had him throw his arms around Hadi's neck. Then they looped the rope around both their waists, pulling it tight. Hadi climbed over the side with Ali strapped to his back and slowly descended the wooden steps of the ladder one by one. "Hold on," Hadi kept telling Ali as his hands slipped from around Hadi's neck.

They arrived on the boat and the crew helped lay Ali on a bench, but he was shaking so violently they thought he might fall off. One of the crew members wrapped him in a mylar blanket though the temperature was warm and rising now that the sun was above the horizon. Ali raised his hand and pointed up to the deck of the ship. He saw his mother bathed in the golden light of the rising sun, standing above the rope ladder as if waiting for some-one to rescue her. The engine of the patrol boat came to life. "No! We cannot leave," he shouted in a hoarse voice. "My mother. You must rescue her."

"No, Ali," said Hadi. "You are seeing things. But I have to go back up the ladder to stay with the ship. I will make sure no one is left behind. Be well my friend."

"But I see her," said Ali, still pointing with a shaky finger. And then a second person, a man with a halo of golden curls in the morning light ap-peared with a hand raised in the air, possibly waving goodbye or calling to be saved. "Eric is there too. We must help him."

"Who's Eric?" said one of the crew members.

"The messman," said Ali.

Hadi shook his head and began climbing the ladder. "*La taqlaq,* my friend. Don't worry. You will be home soon."

As he followed Hadi's climb up the ladder, other people appeared on the deck of the ship—a little girl and a woman. "They are all there," he said.

"You are going home, Ali," a crew member said again as the boat pulled away.

Everybody kept saying home. Home? He had no home. His mother, wife, and daughter were gone. His friend was gone.

Ali began to cry, which quickly turned to weeping, not for the relief of being off the ship or the end to his two-year ordeal, not because he would soon be sleeping in clean sheets and eating the food he dreamed about. He wept for the home he was leaving, the big hulk of a ship getting smaller and smaller as the boat approached land. How could he be pleased now that they, his loved ones, would be prisoners of the ship as he was? He felt as if he had been stripped of his skin and his heart ripped out. At least, on the ship, he had his visitors. In the real world, he would be nothing but a broken man.

COMMUNION

MICHAEL ALENYIKOV

First published under the name Michael Stuart Allen in *Bloom: A thoroughly queer literary journal*, 1999.

Roger wants us to go away for a week. I do not. He's collected brochures for bed and breakfasts. He's maxed his Gold Visa card with its shimmering silver hologram: on camping equipment, a kite, cross country skis, and snorkeling gear. They fill his once tidy apartment, totems to Roger's simple faith in our future. Together.

Roger loves the outdoors. "For me, it's like church," he says.

Maybe if we take a trip he'll be distracted and we won't fight.

For weeks he's been saying we're losing the intimacy thing. What's it look like I'd say? If it's a thing, what's its shape, its color, its size? Where'd we leave it? I'd ask, egging him on, imagining something warm to the touch, soft like velvet, bordello red and sticky with Velcro; too large to misplace in a drawer or closet; too obvious of value to throw out by mistake with the trash.

"Let's go somewhere, *anywhere*," he coos, ignoring my taunts, licking the inside of my ear. "Let's do something totally dorky, like go to the Pocanos."

"No way," I say, "It's too cold. And, besides, I want to stay home and read, in bed, with you."

"We'll watch *The Bitter Tears of Petra Von Kant* again. You know we will," he says and holds his hands out towards me, palms up, like a supplicating saint, eagerness and innocence stamped on his face.

I'm drowning in him and wonder: is the same as love?

I can't say for sure how we decided to go fly a kite on Fire Island: a day trip, an edgy compromise.

We set out on an oddly warm December Saturday. The sun, a pale winter disk with the look of a communion wafer, hugs the horizon, early in its low winter arc across the sky. A twitchy Citibank sign reads seventy degrees.

Nervous euphoria unsettles the faces of people on the street. It's expressed in tentative smiles and furtive glances; a conspiracy of unspoken hope that this year winter might never arrive, leavened with a wariness of being taken in, of being made fools of once again.

We walk along East 7th Street towards Avenue A. I follow Roger, whose long loping strides gather such momentum I think he might take flight. The image of a giraffe with wings, a mutant angel, one of god's sillier failed experiments, takes shape in my mind. The red and black Chinese dragon kite dances behind him.

On Avenue A Roger hails a cab and we stuff ourselves into the smell of synthetic pine cones. Roger says to the cabby, "Penn Station," and I say to Roger, "We could have walked." Without turning his head to look at me he says, "This is just great, don't worry."

I say, "Oh really?" and struggle to remember some detail I love about him: the feel of our legs entwined in bed; the way when I'm lonely, he'd startle me with an unexpected touch; the steady rhythmic sound of his breathing while he slept, a silky thread that, lying awake at night, I'd follow, thinking it would lead me to some safe, secure place, whose terrain I'd imagined he knew far better than me.

The ferry to the Island is half full; men, mostly, with fading tans and perfect haircuts. In the austere winter light, I conjure ghosts, and the boat feels haunted. Roger's dark-tinted glasses mask his eyes. I can see my reflection: small, distant, like looking the wrong way through binoculars, and queasy doubts seep into me with the wind's damp salty spray.

On the dock we hop off and follow the smell of salt and sea to the beach. Solitary men with sculpted chests, each identical, stroll past. Roger and I love the beach but we're not Fire Island types. Our modest pecs are square enough, but there's a lack of precision, a lack of rigor to our cooking and place settings, our clothes, our careers and, I'd always assumed, to our clunky and passionate love making. For the first time I wonder if Roger made love differently with the men he was with before me. I take his hand. He gives me a puzzled look. Until now, it had been his job to take *my* hand, to reassure.

The beach is empty. Walking along the water's edge with Roger and our kite, my mood improves. We make sense, yes, we do; the whole *is* greater than the sum of its parts. We could live together; we *could* be happy.

Roger runs along the beach with the kite. Sand flies out from beneath his feet. I struggle to keep up. The kite gains height, then falls. But Roger, patient in a way I could never be, yanks purposefully on the string. The kite bounces in the air but each time the wind fails it.

"Let me try," I say, but he shakes me off. His patience, I'm reminded, is built, when I least expect it, on a headstrong determination to go it alone. Finally, with Roger dancing on his toes, wind and speed take the kite aloft. He runs in loops and circles, hooting and hollering, his face, a drunken smile of joy. The kite soars ever higher, a small dark speck, mingling with the heavens.

Roger seems to offer me the string but doesn't completely let go and for a moment we're both pulling on the line. "Let go," I say tersely, and he does. Roger says he wants to live with me, that he needs me, but when I watch him at times like these, he seems to be in his own private playground and I realize how much like a prop I feel, like I could be anyone, that he could come alive as easily in the eyes of any other man.

The kite suddenly dips. I pull on the string to gain control but it snaps and bucks in the wind. Roger grabs my hand roughly. "For Chrissake give it some slack. Let it fly. Let it fly free," he says, tightening his grip on my hand until I shake him off. "You hold on to everything too tight, that's your problem," he says. "Sometimes I can't feel myself breathe when I'm with you." His forehead and mouth tighten in anger. I step backward, my feet and calves slapped by the cold surf, and watch as the anger becomes rage, which sweeps across his face with the abruptness of a flash flood. When it subsides he looks sheepish, startled at his own intensity

Hurt and confused, I wonder: why does he wants to live with me if I'm so suffocating?

We walk along the shore. The kite trails aimlessly behind me. The silence deepens recklessly.I feel connected to Roger by an invisible rope, one end knotted in my stomach the other in his; the knots pulling on our guts.

I don't know what he wants; what I don't want is this.

The clouds have become thicker, more deeply gray; in the distance, a soft rumble. Roger trips on a piece of driftwood and stumbles, breaking his fall with his hands. I look away, embarrassed by this revelation of his newfound clumsiness.

Suddenly, he tugs on my shirt.

"Enough kites for one day," he says. The old Roger is back, and he slips the string from my hand into his. "Let this one go free," he whoops, jumping up and down. The kite hovers indecisively in the wind, then turns its back on us and is sucked up into the sky.

"Let's do it in the dunes," he says and next, hidden by some bushes, we're rolling in the sand like it's real summer, not this faux stuff. "We've never made love outdoors," he says as he slides my shirt off. "And *it is* our ninth anniversary," he adds, unbuckling my belt.

"Nine months," we cry in unison as I roll him over on his stomach and separate him from his clothes. Then, beginning with the toes of his left foot, I run my tongue the length of his long skinny body avoiding the patches of light and dark crusted sand that have stuck to his skin. He tastes of sweat– oily, pungent, salty like sardines.

When I reach the back of his neck he flips over and grips my head in his hands. "We could live together, you know, like an experiment," he says and I imagine a mad scientist's laboratory with foaming vials. "We can always be roommates if it doesn't work out," he adds, a touch of pleading in his voice.

"You sound desperate," I say and feel cruel. Our arms and legs become entangled like a pretzel and I try to feel where exactly I begin and Roger leaves off. In the process of searching one of us lets go and we fall apart.

He lays his face on my lap and sucks like a child, then stops and looks up. "I want you inside of me," he says, softly. He reaches for his pants, digs into a pocket, then hands me a rubber. This is the first time Roger has let me fuck him.

Inside of him now, I am in love: with his smooth sweaty back, the shape of his butt, the hair on his thin legs that ends abruptly midway up his each thigh, like a line of showers in a distant spring storm. I can feel Roger's doubt; about me, about us, and that feeling is exhilarating.

"I love the nape of your neck," I whisper in his ear and he turns his head to say "Slower, you're hurting me."

Then he rolls us over and I'm looking into his eyes. "I need to know soon," he says.

"Know what?"

"Whether you want to live with me."

I start to pull out. "Don't," he says with a whimper that shocks me with its nakedness. "I need to know, I just do," he says; and, as if in reply to his question, feeling his warm, uneven breath on my neck, his hands clutching, slipping, searching my back for patches of sand and mud, for traction, I sink even more deeply into him.

Moments later, Roger comes with a long sigh and a smooth hum; I follow, sputtering like an old Chevy. The wind rustles crackling ferns and scraggly grasses, blowing sand into darting whirlwinds around us. Rain begins to fall, a steady drumbeat of large, warm, wet drops, landing on sand, on skin: the sounds of intimacy, so close.

Selected Poetry

Kelliane Parker

MEET YOU AT TAU HERCULID

Crumbling trails across the sky
writing love letters…
the universe applauded our longing

What is natural phenomenon?

A spectacular alchemy
the monas hieroglyphica smiled
at the universal secret

What if Mercury did it's bide?
or Venus clam-shelled on Neptune's shore?
What if Jupiter's moons applauded?

Savored this super nova
This lachrymal baptism
of tidal waves

The way our moon-hearts beat
to the lunar tides
of opening ourselves up to

All the possibilities
All the wonder
All the beauty

Of a dying comet's
last words
and you

My Zenith

"No one has imagined us. We want to live like trees, sycamores blazing through the sulfuric air, dappled with scars, still exuberantly budding, our animal passion rooted in the city." –Adrienne Rich

GIRL GETS GIRL

The best pick-up line
Is a broken heart
Still beating

Who can resist the urge
To stop the bleeding
Tend wounds

There, there love

Our need to love
Is as urgent as the need to
Be loved

So, if you want to get the girl
Open your sternum
And say,

It hurts…right here

The word *erotica* is synonymous with *divine feminine*. It is where consent, body autonomy, body positivity convenes with sexual liberation. When queer and lesbian women connect, whether for a night or a lifetime, we both push limits and hold boundaries.

ALONE WITH YOU

Your hair traces love poems
Across my breasts, down my arms
Gravity holds this brush of you
And we in tangled knots
Of yours and mine and yours
The faint tracing and mapping
Of favorites places in you and me
Of whispered moans
Of a secret language
One shared only on our lips
Of lips on lips, tender
The tenderness of you
Warm and deep
The juicy, strawberry tongue
Opens torrential flows
Of intoxicating waterfalls
Pouring every color, every flower
Of clenching and arching
And fountain releasing
Raining your beauty on me
Bathed in the heady scents
The gift of you left behind

About the Authors

M.D. Neu

Growing up in an accepting family author M.D. Neu always wondered why there were never stories reflecting our diverse queer society. Surrounded by characters that only mirrored heterosexual society, he decided to change that and began writing, wanting to tell epic stories that reflect our varied world. Over the years, Neu has written several Urban Fantasy, Science Fiction, and Paranormal works. His Science Fiction novels *A New World-Contact* and *Conviction* won the 2018-2019 International Rainbow Awards: Best Gay Alternative Universe/Reality & Sci-Fi / Futuristic books. Recently, his novella *T.A.D.-The Angel of Death* won the 2020-2021 International Rainbow Awards: Best Gay Alternative Universe/Reality and was one of the Runner Ups for Best Gay Book. Neu's debut novel, *The Calling*, was featured in the *San Jose Mercury News* (January 2018) garnering him national recognition. When not writing M.D. Neu works for a non-profit in Silicon Valley and travels with his husband of twenty-plus years.

R.L. Merrill

R.L. Merrill brings you stories of Hope, Love, and Rock 'n' Roll featuring quirky and relatable characters. Whether she's writing contemporary, paranormal, or supernatural, she loves to give readers a shiver with compelling stories that will stay with you long after. You can find her connecting with readers on social media, advocating for America's youth, raising two brilliant teenagers, writing horror-infused music reviews for HorrorAddicts.net, trying desperately to get that back piece finished in the tattoo chair, or headbanging at a rock show near her home in the San Francisco Bay Area! Stay tuned for more Rock 'n' Romance.

Liz Faraim

Liz Fariam has a full plate between balancing a day job, parenting, writing, and finding some semblance of a social life. In past lives, she has been a soldier, a bartender, a shoe salesperson, an assistant museum curator, and even a driving instructor. She focuses her writing on strong, queer, female leads who don't back down. Liz transplanted to California from New York over thirty years ago, and now lives in the East Bay Area. She enjoys exploring nature with her wife and son.

K.S. Trenten

K.S. Trenten lives in the South Bay area with her husband, two cats, and a crowd of characters in her head; all shouting for attention. Follow K.S. Trenten, locate her published works, or read free samples at…

Facebook

http://www://facebook.com/rhodrymavelyne/

Twitter

https://twitter.com/rhodrymavelyne

Goodreads

https://www.goodreads.com/author/show/14876500.K_S_Trenten

Amazon Author Page

http://www.amazon.com/author/kstrenten

Nine Star Press Author Page

https://ninestarpress.com/authors/k-s-trenten/

The Cauldron of Eternal Inspiration

http://www://inspirationcauldron.wordpress.com

WAYNE GOODMAN

Wayne Goodman has lived in the San Francisco Bay Area most of his life (with too many cats). Goodman hosts Queer Words Podcast, conversations with queer-identified authors about their works and lives. When not writing or recording, he enjoys playing Gilded Age parlor music on the piano, with an emphasis on women, gay, and Black composers.

RICHARD MAY

Richard May writes Gay fiction. His work has appeared in numerous literary journals, story anthologies, and his collections *Ginger Snaps: Photos & Stories of Redheaded Queer People, Inhuman Beings,* and *Gay All Year: Twelve Stories.* He is a member of the18th Street Writers and the Bay Area Queer Writers Association. Rick organizes the Odd Mondays and Perfectly Queer reading series. He lives in San Francisco.

GAR McVEY-RUSSELL

Gar's first novel, *Sin Against the Race* (gamr books, 2017) was listed on The Advocate's Best Books We Read in 2018: LGBTQ Novels. His short stories, *Tom of Boalt Hall* and *The Necklace* were finalists in the Saints and Sinners LGBTQ Festival Fiction Open in 2020 and 2022, respectively. His fiction has also appeared in *Sojourner: Black Gay Voices in the Age of AIDS* (1993) and *Harrington Gay Men's Fiction Quarterly* (vol. 7, Num. 3, 2005). He publishes a blog, *the gar spot.* Gar is married and lives in Oakland, California, where he listens to a lot of jazz.

Vincent Traughber Meis

Vincent Traughber Meis is a fiction writer, a world traveler, and a former ESL community college teacher. When he's not traveling, he divides his time between writing and working in the garden. He has published six novels: *Eddie's Desert Rose, Tio Jorge, Down in Cuba, Deluge, Four Calling Burds* and *The Mayor of Oak Street. Tio Jorge, Down in Cuba,* and *Deluge* have all won Rainbow Awards and *The Mayor of Oak Street* a Reader Views Reviewer's Choice Award. His short stories have been appeared in several collections both in print and online. One of his stories was a finalist in the Saints and Sinners Short Fiction Contest 2021. A collection of short stories, *Far from Home,* was published in October 2021. He lives in San Leandro, California.

Michael Alenyikov

Michael Alenyikov is the pen name for the author of *Ivan and Misha*, which received the Northern CA Book Award for fiction and the Gina Berriault Award from SF State. It was also a Finalist for the Edmund White Award for Debut Fiction. His writing has been widely published in such journals as *Foglifter, The Forge,* the *James White Review,* the *Catamaran Literary Reader,* the *Gay & Lesbian Review* and many others. He's a New York City native and long-time resident of San Francisco. Michael is a former clinical psychologist who retired early after becoming disabled with a neuro immune disorder.

Kelliane Parker

Kelliane Parker is a queer, Latinx Bay Area poet and the author of, *Down the Foggy Streets of My Mind,* from Nomadic Press. Her work focuses on healing from trauma and living with Dissociative Identity Disorder. She very proud to be a new member of the Bay Area Queer Writers Association, (BAQWA). Kelliane has been featured in numerous anthologies including the recent Lawrence Ferlinghetti tribute anthology, *Light on the Walls of Life,* edited by Bobby Coleman. You can find her performing all over the Bay Area and Zoomlandia.

All proceeds from this limited-time anthology will be donated to the Lavender Library and Archives in Sacramento, California.